Anamnesis

History of Sol Book 2

Steven Dutch, Chris Masterton

Masterton Dutch Multimedia

Copyright © 2021

Steven Dutch & Chris Masterton

All rights reserved.

History of Sol

Book 3: Second Edition

iii

Written by

Steven Dutch & Chris Masterton

Edited by

'Mick'

Cover art by

Jason Giraldo

Cover design and formatting by

Chris Masterton

Acknowledgements

Since starting out on this journey a number of years ago, we have met some really awesome people. The biggest influence of all has been a bloke called Mick, who reached out to us with a helping hand after we released the first edition of book 1. We are better writers because of his patience, feedback, and attention to detail.

Massive thanks go to Jason for another fantastic cover, helping bring out visions to life, and to Amanda for help with formatting. Shout out to Marie (for bringing the snacks) and Amanda for being great company at the conferences.

Like most authors, we have some very understanding partners, Rach and Yani, who accept that we need to be glued to our computer screens for hours on end and are always there for emotional support.

Finally, all the fans who have read, enjoyed, and even loved our books; thank you for coming to meet us at the conventions, giving us feedback, and for supporting our journey!

This book is dedicated to Michael Dutch

26/10/1988 - 22/06/2016

DATAFILE

Matias-1 Orbital Space Station

NODE 1

The *Matias-1* (*M1*) Space Station is one of twelve orbital biospheres constructed as observation platforms orbiting Lunar. The viewing portals look out over the Terranean Expanse, an asteroid belt thought to be the remains of the ancient homeworld.

Originally constructed in cycle 803 (SE), *M1* is the oldest space station still in operation. Although it has received many upgrades and refurbishments over the span of its service, the shell and core structure of the station remain the same.

NODE 2

Aurora City is the main platform of *M1*. Home to 2.8 million Lunarians who live and work on the station. The city is topped by the Observation Decks and an operations platform, which serve as a historical monument to the homeworld. Aurora is viewed by the Lunarians as one of the best places to live in the Colonies.

NODE 3

The laser lifts connect the city of Aurora to the Observation Decks by using a concentrated column of light to levitate large circular platforms up and down the centre of the station. It was originally designed as a security measure to protect the Observation Decks, which held relics from the remnants of the homeworld. This is now considered something of a novelty, as this technology is not used on any other space station.

Aurora City.
Your Home
Among The Stars
Matias Orbital Platforms brought to you by the Lunar Colony

CHAPTER ONE

Final Shift - C1099 S5 R2

Civic Armin felt the electric pulse surge through his brain, waking him instantly. He reached out and grabbed his Link, which drifted in front of him. Rubbing his eyes, he looked at the display. It was almost time for his work shift in the control centre. He knew it would be busy, so he cleared his mind to focus on his primary objective. People of extremely high Value from all over the Colonies would be meeting on the Observation Decks to take part in the ancient tradition of the Anamnesis, where they commemorated the mistakes made in the distant past that resulted in the destruction of the homeworld. He didn't really believe any of that garbage. Stories like that were always being told to keep everyone in the Colonies obedient and suppressed.

He peeled the neural stimulator from his forehead, deactivated the suspension field and floated gracefully to the floor. The hatch hissed open and he stepped out of his cramped rejuvenation chamber, pausing to neaten his hair and moustache in the tiny mirror on the wall.

He hated waking up this way. The idea of his mind being turned on and off by a machine felt like a complete violation. Sure, it was easy and efficient, but it still felt wrong. Luckily, it would be his last time on board the *M1* Orbital Space Station. This rotation was going to be a big one and he couldn't wait for it to be over. After eight sub-cycles of tolerating this suppression and turmoil, he would finally get to go home and see his family.

The outer crew chamber wasn't much less confined than his rejuvenation chamber. Which upon exiting, placed him directly across from his bunkmate, Samuel 'Brute' Rennom. Brute was already awake and had begun the daily struggle to cram his muscular torso into a standard issue uniform.

"You know what I'll miss about these sleep coffins?" Brute grumbled.

Civic decided to humour him. "Is it the claustrophobia?"

"No. I like waking up in the mornings and not desperately needing to take a piss."

Civic forced a weak grin. "Are you ready for this, Brute?"

Brute nodded slowly, likely deep in thought about what they were going to do. His reply was almost insightful. "Soon, we will become mighty heroes. For better or worse, we will be the ones that people remember in times to come. After all, this is our destiny!"

"Well said," Civic agreed. "Let's go."

He led the way out into the communal area, where Pulse and Lannek were already waiting for them. Lannek drained a tube of Organix as they entered and casually tossed it across the stark room into the waste hatch on the wall. Pulse watched the tube's arc from his perch atop a bulky machine; a black cube with chrome handles on each side, fronted by an interface.

"Why are you still drinking that nasty slush?" Pulse asked. "Just stop by the galley like I did and swipe some real food while those mindless fools aren't looking. They've already got the good stuff out for the event."

Lannek let out an almighty belch and grinned from ear to ear. "I like the way it tastes."

Civic shook his head. "If you drink enough of that stuff you'll become one of them." He turned to Pulse. "Did you get what I asked for?"

Pulse nodded, fumbled through his pocket, and retrieved four black wristbands. He placed one around his own wrist and snapped it closed. It beeped as it locked in place. He threw the others to Civic, Brute and Lannek.

Civic secured his wristband, then looked over at the black and chrome cube supporting Pulse's thin frame. "So that's the frequency generator? Did you have any trouble getting it?"

"Nope," Pulse said. "It was exactly where our friend said it would be. Everyone is so busy with the Anamnesis that we went largely unnoticed. I think this is going to be cinch."

Civic closed his eyes and put a hand on Brute's shoulder. "May the light of Sol shine on us this Rotation." He opened his eyes, the others still stood in silent prayer of their own. "Well then, we all know what we have to do. Let's get to it, shall we?"

Brute pushed Pulse off the machine and, with a grunt, he lifted it up to his chest using the two chrome handles. He gave a nod and they headed for the service passages.

The corridors were dull, narrow, and dimly lit. They contrasted sharply with the ornate lavishness of the ancient space station's public areas. Strangely, they didn't encounter any other workers on their way.

Civic activated his Link and keyed in an audio connection. "Glitch, it's Civ. Are you at the laser lifts yet?"

A soft feminine voice replied, but her words were short and to the point. "On our way to the lifts now. Are you guys ready?" She sounded tense. Which was understandable, given the nature of their mission, but he had to make sure her head was in the right place.

"We are," he said. "Everything is in place. Are you alright?"

"We're fine," she answered.

"Stay focused. No more Link connections from this point on. Stick to the timeline." When she didn't acknowledge, he added, "this is the will of the Divine. We will prevail!"

"May the light of Sol shine on us," she said, and then cut the connection.

Only the sound of footsteps could be heard as they conspicuously made their way towards the top level. It seemed to take forever to reach the destination, which was only a brisk walk up two floors from their lodgings.

They looked up at the large thick doors that stood between them and their fate. Civic placed his hand on the interface beside the control centre door and lights within the door frame flashed from red to green.

"Remember, in and out, just like we planned," Civic whispered.

Every time Civic set foot in the control centre, he felt like he was stepping into outer space due to the transparent walls of the expansive dome-shaped enclosure. The whole area was lit by rows of older style flat-panel interfaces. They were complemented by a silver glow from the Lunar surface, the shimmer from the cities of towering skyscrapers far below, too small to see with the naked eye. He wondered which city would be most affected by the events about to take place.

"Quit stargazing!" The Station Commander snapped. "We've got a lot of important guests here. Get to your post and make sure this old pot keeps spinning."

"Sir!" Civic saluted hastily and hurried over to his station. He looked around at the ten other workers standing at various posts around him, going about their duties. They were like mindless drones, with no purpose but to serve the Colonies. Pulse took up a station across from him. Lannek and Brute entered after them and moved around the back. Brute struggled with the cumbersome generator.

The Station Commander eyed Lannek and Brute impatiently. "Who are you lot?"

"We're from the surface," Brute replied with a forced Lunarian accent. "We're here to fix the broken interface. Work order's in the system. You needed specialty parts."

The commander gave them a look that said he really didn't care and had far more important things to concern himself with. "Hurry up then," he said dismissively.

Brute and Lannek exchanged a look and put their tools down by the interface that Civic had broken several rotations earlier. Brute sighed with relief and wiped the sweat from his forehead with his sleeve. He checked his wristband as he watched them, ensuring it was still tightly fastened.

Lannek opened a panel on the floor and attached one heavy-duty power node to the frequency generator and another to the broken interface. A surge of electricity shot through the entire chamber the moment the connector click-locked into place. Lightning arced across the room, crackling from every metal surface. The Operators' bodies all stiffened at once. Sparks flickered across their limbs, torsos, and heads. Error messages flashed across all the interfaces, drowning the room in a crimson glow. Civic's wristband lit up, absorbing the shock, as did those of his crew.

The Station Commander's eyes widened. He opened his mouth in a silent scream before collapsing. One of the workers grabbed Brute by the arm. The brief contact was enough to redirect the current into Brute's wristband. This bought the control centre operator a few additional seconds of life. Probably only long enough to realise what was going on. Eyes wide with panic, he threw a desperate punch. Brute deflected the blow with ease and grabbed the operator by the neck, depriving him of air. His legs thrashed as Brute shook him violently. The kicking and squirming continued. Then he gurgled and eventually stopped moving. Brute threw him effortlessly against an interface, and he slid to the ground with a thud.

Civic surveyed the bodies scattered throughout the dome.

"Well, that was easy," Lannek remarked.

"I told you," Civic said with an uneasy grin. "Now let's get to work."

Lannek wrenched the power-node connector out from the broken interface. The crimson light dissipated, and the room returned to normal.

"I'm into the thruster systems now," Pulse said. "Getting ready to give this baby a push."

"Hope you know what you're doing," Brute grumbled.

"I got this," Pulse reassured them. "Civic might be our brave leader, but you need tech-savvy, you talk to me."

The frequency generator lit with a purple glow as it powered up.

"Jamming frequency's broadcasting," Civic confirmed, his fingers dancing across the console. "By the time anyone realises what's happening, it'll be too late. Their Links will be completely useless." He looked up. "Pulse, have you detected the explosions yet?"

"No... but I should have." Pulse was tapping frantically at the interface. Panic threatened his calm resolve. "Do you think something went wrong with the explosives?"

"Shit... I hope not." Brute scratched the back of his neck. He had been in charge of putting together the detonators. "The laser lifts were supposed to go off before the thrusters, that was the plan. Scrub and Glitch knew that. So why haven't the lifts exploded yet?"

"I'm sure she is at the lifts," Civic said, trying to reassure them. "Maybe they hit a snag. They'll get it done, any moment now. Nobody's leaving the Observation Decks any time soon, have faith, my friend."

The station rumbled and shook as the thrusters broke *M1*'s orbit around Lunar. Alarms sounded, but the four saboteurs ignored them.

"People must have felt that," Lannek said. "Let's get out of here."

After they left their stations and reached the exit, Brute raised his pulse rifle and shot a burst through each of the interfaces. "Let's see them try to stop us now!"

"Stop wasting time," Civic scowled. "Let's go, we need to meet up with Glitch and Scrub, then we are home free!"

But none of them moved. They all just stood there, staring out into the image of the void displayed on the dome behind him.

Civic had assigned Lannek the task of hacking into the escape pod protocols so that when they launched, all the other pods would go with them. This would leave everyone else stranded onboard. Unable to use the lifts. Unable to escape. Condemning them to suffer the same fate as the ancient space station.

So what he saw when he turned around chilled him to the bone. There he was, frozen in place, looking up at the live-feed image of the escape pods drifting away without them.

Lannek grabbed Brute by the collar and shook him. "You idiot! What have you done? You just had to shoot the interfaces, didn't you? You've screwed us all, you moron!"

Brute pushed Lannek away effortlessly. "I'm no idiot moron. You're the idiot moron who rigged the damn escape pods. You did it wrong!"

Lannek ran at Brute screaming, but Civic got between them.

"That's enough!" He yelled. "Don't be foolish, either of you! There is no way to know for sure why the escape pods launched prematurely. If we want to get off this godforsaken death trap alive, we need to keep our heads. Right now, it doesn't matter whose fault it was. We need to get to Glitch and Scrub and hope that by the light of Sol they still haven't blown the laser lifts yet."

"Of course they've blown the laser lifts," Lannek shouted. "It was all part of your genius fucking master plan. Now we're all going to die here!"

"Pull yourself together man," Civic said. "Pulse, talk to me, what can we do here?"

Pulse was sitting on the ground with his head buried in his knees in the brace position. He looked up at them in a daze. "There is nothing we can do. The interfaces are shot, the escape pods are gone, the laser lifts have likely been destroyed by now. This is our fate, the will of the Divine. We cannot take so many lives without paying this ultimate price."

They all paused, with nothing but the rumbling of the station and the sound of the alarms.

"No! I refuse to give up," Civic said, trying to force hope into his tone. "We are doing this by the will of The Divine, for the good of Sol, so we *will* get off this bloody station or die trying!"

DATAFILE

The Nexus

"War has always been the driving force behind the Colonies. If we are to survive, we need to find a new reason to work, develop and grow together, instead of against each other." - Peacekeeper Chronius Saxon

NODE 1

After the homeworld was destroyed, humans colonised the solar system. For hundreds of cycles, two factions fought to establish dominance. After many cycles of war, two other factions emerged from mining outposts further from the sun. Eventually, the Nexus Peace Treaty was established in the interest of system-wide cooperation and resource sharing. So a collective of Peacekeepers was formed to represent all the Colony nations as one. This sparked the first unified project to collaborate on a universal communication and data sharing network known simply as Nexus.

NODE 2

Each Colony appoints three Peacekeepers (Proper) to form the Nexus Council, which is situated on Mars. The Council is supported by an understudy of Peacekeepers In-Guidance and administered by Colony Representatives. Once an individual becomes a Peacekeeper, their life contract with a Colony is absolved, so that they can remain neutral and unbiased to act in the best interest of the Nexus.

NODE 5

Subsection 12 - Minor conflicts between no more than two colonies for up to one cycle, where neither Colony is directly attacked by more than three ships are not considered an act of war violating the treaty. However, mediation is required by the Peacekeepers to end the dispute.

CHAPTER TWO

Dilemma

Clarissa pushed gently past a knot of elaborately uniformed diplomats and waved away a robotoid carrying a variety of exotic hors d'oeuvres. People smiled at her as she passed, which made her feel like the centre of attention. Everyone knew who Clarissa Dalton was; the daughter of Peacekeeper John Dalton—the leader who saved them from the Cyborgs.

Her holographic dress glimmered in the lights. They were the latest trend; billions of tiny particles projected around her body that were dense enough to feel like real material keeping her covered. The design was made to look like blue opaque glass wrapped elegantly around her body, but it flowed, moved, and felt like silk. Rare gems, gifts from her father, hung from her ears and neck.

The rabble of a hundred conversations pressed at her. Accents and dialects from all four colonies merging into a blanket of noise. She caught occasional words, the odd phrase; some was gossip, some was colonial politics, a lot was newcomers idly marvelling at the view beyond the lounge's high, clear walls. Two representatives from the Jupiter Alliance debated angrily over the nature of the asteroid belt known as the Terranean Expanse and its rumoured beginnings as the homeworld.

"Clarissa! Over here! Clarissa!" a voice called over the noise.

She looked around and her heart sank at the sight of Eryn Jaines manoeuvring through the crowd towards her.

Eryn was almost the same age as her and was quite an attractive young gentleman. He wore what looked like a stylised military uniform merged with a plant. Colourful red, blue, and orange leaves flowed elegantly around his midsection and wrapped its way down his trousers. He had always been obsessed with her. Finding any chance to speak to or sit next to her at social events. It was even worse that their fathers were long-time acquaintances, so it made him difficult to avoid.

"Eryn, how lovely to see you again," Clarissa said with forced politeness.

"Of course it is," he said, embracing her in a hug that was a bit too intimate and then held it for a little too long. "I knew I would run into you here. I've been looking forward to it. I have some wonderful news to tell you! As you may have heard, I am under consideration for the role of Supreme Commander of the new space fleet for my father's Advancement Entity."

"Supreme Commander?" Clarissa gasped." But you're not even a soldier! Besides, I thought Ryan Swift was the Supreme Commander."

"Yes, my dear. That is because currently, the Martian fleet is the largest. But when the Martians pay tribute to the UAE as part of the pending agreement, and I am accepted as its leader, then I will have the largest military in all of Sol. Therefore, I will be the Supreme Commander."

"*You* will have the largest military? That's awfully presumptuous isn't it?"

"I believe I have a lot to offer. Youth, power, a keen mind. The only thing I don't have is a unity with a strong, capable woman."

"I'm surprised you're stopping at one," Clarissa said through her forced smile.

She always thought the idea of a polyamorous relationship detracted from the passion of a unity, whereby two people would be the one-and-only for each other. She knew it was an old and outdated notion, but still longed for the idea of true, undivided love.

Eryn took her hand in both of his. "There is only one woman I want, Clarissa. We have known each other for so long, our families have strong ties and excellent positions, and we have so much in common!"

Clarissa scrunched her nose, an expression she knew her father hated her making. She fought to hide her revulsion.

"Let's face it," he said smugly. "You'd have a tough time finding a better match."

"Would I now? Maybe I don't want a unity with you." Then, remembering their social protocol, said, "have you broached this matter with my father?"

"No," he admitted. "And don't tease me like that. I know you don't mean it."

She felt a moment of slight relief that this could just be a fancy of his, rather than a well-prepared plan.

"Having said that," he continued airily. "I believe our fathers are discussing the matter at this very moment."

Clarissa suddenly felt her heart drop. The room whirled around her and she desperately wanted to sit down. The tightness in her chest and throat made it hard to breathe. She had to find her father immediately.

"Eryn, I am flattered by your bold proposition. However, I must consult my father about this. Please, if you would excuse me, I must go and find him at once."

"Of course, my dear," he said with a smile and a wink. "I will see you at dinner."

Clarissa turned away and pushed on without looking back. She pulled her Link from the holographic dress and typed a quick message to her father, insisting that she needed to speak with him urgently.

A hand grasped her shoulder. She tensed, expecting Eryn to be following her like a lost puppy. To her relief, it was her friend June, the Commander of the Lunar fleet.

"June! It's wonderful to see you. I was just on my way to speak with my father about something important. Could I catch up with you afterwards?"

"Actually, I was hoping to speak with you before I left the station," June said. "I've been called back to Lunar due to a glitch in our defence grid, something to do with the auto-targeting protocols. But anyway, I have some concerns about the United Advancement Entity that I feel need to be represented here and I was hoping you could officiate?"

Clarissa considered the odd request. Was it related to Eryn's new appointment? Could Eryn's ambitions to form a unity with her have spread so quickly that even June already knew of it?

"Surely such a big issue could be raised by a Peacekeeper Proper," Clarissa suggested. "Or even a Lunar Representative?"

"I hope they will, but I need you to back this for me. I think it would mean a lot more coming from a Dalton. You may not like it, but your family has a lot of influence."

Clarissa glanced over at where she thought her father might be conversing and checked her Link for a reply. Still nothing.

"How much do you know about the UAE?" June asked.

"Well, it's a new Colony initiative. I know that we are terraforming Umbriel and Oberon to support human habitation. Though it will be cold that far out—"

"No. I mean, why have we been asked by the Nexus to tribute massive amounts of resources and a third of our military for a new colony? What's out there that's so important? If each Colony is contributing equally then the UAE will have a dominating force."

Clarissa shook her head. "Why does this worry you? Currently, Mars has the largest fleet and that isn't any cause for concern, but—"

"So far they have upheld the peace," June agreed. "But a shift of power like this for no apparent reason could only mean trouble."

This grated Clarissa. The Nexus were the ones upholding the peace, not Mars.

"I suspect the Nexus feels as though the new colony will need protection as it develops," Clarissa said, trying to remain objective.

"From what exactly? The Saturn Alliance consists of a bunch of mining outposts. Outlaws are just a scattered band of human scum playing pirates, preying on ships that wander too far out—"

Clarissa tried to interrupt, but June kept going.

"—or maybe we should be afraid of mutants? They're nothing but myths told by miners to scare others away from taking their resources."

"Are you saying the Nexus has ulterior motives?"

June folded her arms. "I am asking you to question what this expansion is truly about. Look at all the candidates that are to be on the board. Most of them either have a military background or attained greater Value from creating weapons and warships. All I'm saying is this doesn't look like a peaceful endeavour."

June was right about all the people involved, which suddenly reminded Clarissa that she may be forced to form a unity with one of them.

"I don't want you to worry, June. As a Peacekeeper, my father will be heavily involved with this expansion. I can assure you he has nothing but the best intentions for all of the Colonies."

June glanced at her Link. "I hope you're right!" She took both of Clarissa's hands in hers. A gesture of their friendship. "I have to go, please look into this for me. I'm counting on you, Clarissa. I think you will make an excellent Peacekeeper."

Clarissa forced a smile and watched June head back to the laser lifts. She looked at her Link. Still no reply from her father. She had to find him before Eryn's father, Arrol, could convince him to administrate a unity for her.

She passed through the seemingly endless sea of people, excusing herself as she darted between conversations. She looked in every direction trying to spot her father among the many unfamiliar faces. The fear rose in her that it may already be too late and then she saw him, standing at the far side of a lounge area reserved for the highest Value elites. He was already engaged in conversation with Arrol.

She pushed past knots of people to get as close as possible without being noticed. Her father would surely spot her out of the crowd, so she decided to make her way up behind them.

As she got closer, she noticed a vacant chair behind him. She sank into it and lowered her head, pretending to be busy on her Link. She had to focus intently to isolate their voices from the rest of the ambient noise of a hundred other conversations going on around her.

"So, High Chancellor," her father said with a hint of amusement. "That's quite a step up for you."

"I couldn't have done it without your support, John. Many thanks."

"Not necessary. I know you will be the best person to represent the UAE." John paused, perhaps to take a sip of synthohol. "And how is your son doing with his application for Fleet Commander?"

"You know Eryn. He is focused, driven and cunning. A sure frontrunner at the Academy. Actually, I think he would make a perfect match for your Clarissa. Don't you think?"

Clarissa clutched her Link compulsively but remained silent. She imagined her father cringing at the proposition.

"You know, a political unity isn't something I ever wanted for my daughter, but I suppose it comes with the territory. Tell me why it should be Eryn?"

"Well, think about it. My son will be the Commander of the largest military fleet in all of Sol, and your Daughter will be a Peacekeeper. What better way to instil trust in the 'Entity?"

Clarissa held her breath.

"Well, Clarissa and Eryn have always been good friends, I often see them sitting together at these sorts of social events. I think you might be onto something here. She might even be happy about it."

Clarissa couldn't believe how quickly her father could justify trading her away for a slight political advantage. He already seemed to have Arrol eating out of the palm of his hand, why would they need a unity with his son as well?

She spun up out of her chair. "Father, there you are. I have been looking everywhere for you!"

"Clarissa, what is the matter? Can't you see I am in the middle of a conversation?"

She smiled apologetically. "Please excuse me Arrol, I certainly didn't mean to be rude. It's just that I must speak to my father, alone."

Her father gave her the look of disapproval that told her she had crossed the line in a big way. She had gone too far to back down now. There was too much at stake.

"Whatever it is, it can wait," John said. "We were actually in the middle of discussing your future as a Peacekeeper, and where that should take you."

"That's what I'm afraid of, Father. I don't want a unity with Eryn! I don't love him... I don't even like him!"

"Not now, Clarissa," John said through gritted teeth.

"Okay then, when? When is an appropriate time to discuss *you* dictating my future for me?"

"Clarissa," Arrol interrupted calmly. "I don't think you should jump to a decision about this right away. Take some time to consider what is being arranged here."

Clarissa folded her arms and waited. Arrol wasted no time in elaborating.

"Creating this new colony is going to cause a great deal of uncertainty," he said. "It would be easy to consider it a threat rather than a necessity. This may very well undermine the peace which the Nexus currently upholds. As a Peacekeeper, this unity will allow you to provide a sense of assurance to the colonies that no one else possibly could."

"Perhaps the colonies wouldn't need so much reassurance if the UAE wasn't taking such a hostile approach to its expansion. Each colony is currently armed to the teeth in fear of the others. How is forming an even bigger fleet by dismantling each of theirs going to make them feel more at ease?"

Her father weighed in using his Peacekeeper tone. The one that gave him authority on any subject he was discussing. "The entire purpose of the Advancement Entity is to defend against the growing outlaw threat. Do you think we can just make an army appear from nothing? We need the colonies to back this move for their own good."

"Outlaws? Why do you need such a force to disband a small group of separatists?"

"They are a much greater force than you think," Arrol said. "They have built a society of their own. Stealing from us was just the beginning. They have outposts in the far reaches, but they want what Martians take for granted. They want clean air and dirt."

"You expect everyone to just believe this? Show me some proof!"

"Clarissa, that's enough," her father snapped. "Neither of us have any reason to deceive you. The outlaws are a real threat. They aren't just attacking remote mining stations anymore. In the last few sub-cycles they have made bold attacks in Martian space."

"Supreme Commander Swift will even attest to this," Arrol added.

"They've attacked Mars? How could—"

"Yes. They commandeered an old Martian warship. It's just lucky that Swift was able to stop them."

A wave of helplessness suddenly enveloped Clarissa. She knew she had lost. Unless she could prove that there was no reason for the UAE, it would be selfish of her to turn down a unity with Eryn. Especially if it gave the Colonies stability and assurance.

She needed to clear her head and try to figure out how to take control of the situation.

"You're right, Arrol," she said with a composure she didn't feel. "I should take some time to consider your proposal. Please excuse me."

Clarissa turned her back on them and walked away. She felt ill. The weight of all the colonies was on her shoulders. She pushed her way through the crowd of people, feeling more trapped and more alone with each moment that passed.

She turned to make sure her father and Arrol were out of sight. Her breathing had become so heavy that she thought she was going to faint. No one seemed to notice. She wanted to be alone, to break down, to let the sorrow and helplessness wash over her. But she couldn't, not here, not with so many people watching.

She stumbled through the crowds and reached out with an open hand to the viewing portal spanning across one whole side of the lounge. It was cold to touch but sturdy, with a handrail at waist height. She grasped it, letting it prop her up. The view of the void always seemed intimidating. Like standing on the edge of a cliff, intensified by the knowledge that there was endless nothingness on the other side of the reinforced glass.

"Try to hold each breath," a smooth female voice said.

"Excuse me?" Clarissa gasped; eyes glancing over the woman standing beside her in an elegant red dress. Straight away she noticed small white metallic contours and iridescent lines running underneath the surface of the woman's skin. Clarissa gasped.

"Just take a deep breath and hold it for a few seconds. It will help calm your nerves."

"You're a cyborg!" Clarissa said, instantly regretting being so forward. But she had to fight to suppress the irrational fear rising up from her stomach.

"Yes, I am," she replied. "My name is Lisa."

"I'm Clarissa." She decided not to give her last name. Just for a moment, she wanted to be only Clarissa. Not the Peacekeeper's daughter. Not the daughter of the man who had lead to the slaughter of this woman's entire race. Just for once, she wanted to have a normal conversation. Free of politics and agendas. She followed Lisa's advice and took a deep breath, held it, and then let it go slowly. Her next breaths started to come easier.

She decided to change the subject. "It's such an amazing view from up here. All those magnificent towering cities, once a barren wasteland of dirt and rocks. I can't even imagine Lunar being just some un-terraformed moon orbiting an ancient homeworld paradise."

"Ancient paradise?"

"Yeah, you know, like the stories. Do you even believe any of that?"

"What reason would I have to doubt it?" Lisa asked with a puzzled expression.

"I just thought that being a cyborg, you might question stuff like that. The whole story of our species evolving on some perfect utopian homeworld, before being destroyed by believers of a divine being, seems so contrived. Now we are being told that their descendants are a threat and are trying to destroy the Colonies? Why would there be people out there whose sole intent is to destroy civilisation?"

Lisa looked out at the void. "Because we made them the enemy. The Colonies cast them out, told them they have no Value and therefore no place in our way of life. How else do you react in that situation?"

"But what possible threat could they pose?" Clarissa asked, regretting her choice of topics. "We have vast numbers and are protected by powerful armed forces! What do these outlaws have that is such a threat to us now?"

"They are ruthless, and they have nothing to lose."

"How do you know? Have you ever met one?" Clarissa asked, hoping she wasn't being too persistent with her barrage of questions.

"I have. He tried to kill me," Lisa admitted casually.

Clarissa was starting to believe that her father and Arrol might be right about the outlaw threat, if even the first stranger she spoke with had a story about them. She pondered that the Nexus may well have been covering it up until now to avert mass panic. "Oh, I'm sorry. That must have been quite a scary experience."

Lisa took a breath as if to say something, but she remained silent.

Clarissa decided to change the subject again. "So then, why are you standing here all alone just staring out into space? Are you waiting for someone?"

Lisa looked down and fidgeted with her fingers. "Yes, but he is always late."

"Well, he must be worth it," Clarissa suggested. The prospect of a love story piqued her interest.

"Really, he isn't," Lisa replied flatly.

"Then why are you waiting for him? You're all dressed up, looking stunning. Why play his game?" Clarissa asked, motioning to Lisa's stylish red dress.

Lisa blushed ever so slightly. "Because I... I don't know." She looked back out at the stars.

"It's okay, I understand," Clarissa said, burning with curiosity. "You don't have to tell me... but who is he, anyway? I can't imagine someone like you letting anyone get under your skin."

"You mean, someone like a cyborg?" Lisa hesitated. "It's Ryan Swift."

"The Martian Fleet Commander?" Clarissa said incredulously. She covered her mouth and looked around. This brought a smile to them both.

"You mean the *Supreme* Commander," Lisa replied with a smirk.

"What could you possibly see in him?"

Lisa listed the reasons, counting with her fingers. "He's handsome, adventurous, and dangerous."

"That doesn't sound too bad."

"He can also be aggressive, vengeful, and egotistical," Lisa continued. "Our relationship is... complicated."

"Well, at least you have a choice of partner. I'm practically being forced into a unity with this obnoxious, vile—" Clarissa realised she was getting quite animated again. Her hands were out in front of her like she was clawing at the air.

"Is that why you were so upset?"

"I always hoped I would be able to fall in love and make my own choices. Not have it forced upon me."

"Don't let something like that determine your happiness. I was with someone I loved," Lisa said. "But it didn't make my life any easier. In fact, it nearly got me killed." She went silent for a moment, then continued. "So why are you going along with it? What does this person have over you?"

"It's my duty, for the greater good of the Colonies," Clarissa said, resigned to the truth of the words.

"It doesn't sound like you're fighting this because you're not in love," Lisa said. "I think you're fighting this because you're not in control. I've chosen not to be with Swift, despite how it might appear. I want him to know I am doing just fine without him."

"If you want to show him you're doing fine without him, stop trying to impress him," Clarissa said with mock scorn. "But you're right. I just need to own this and take control of the situation. Maybe I should go to Oberon with Eryn and find out what sort of threat these outlaws really pose."

DATAFILE

United Advancement Entity

NODE 1

The United Advancement Entity (UAE) was initiated by the Nexus to provide a first line of defence against the growing threat of outlaw attacks. Outposts were established on two of Uranus' moons (Umbriel and Oberon), with patrols and weapons platforms set up along the planet's orbital path.

The UAE Project proposal called for all colonies to hand over one-third of their military as tribute to the alliance. This would have formed the most powerful fleet in all the Colonies to defeat the outlaws before they managed to gain a greater foothold in the outer reaches of Sol.

NODE 8

Archival records from terraforming older colonies (such as Lunar and Mars) in the distant past reveal that it is possible, with the use of highly guarded technology, to change the gravitational and electromagnetic fields of a celestial body. Devices known as Seeds were deployed to create a series of artificial gravimetric fields which control atmospheric conditions. Genetically engineered plant life is introduced to cultivate a breathable atmosphere which protects against ultraviolet solar radiation, as well as warming and maintaining the surface temperatures for habitation.

CHAPTER THREE

Gala

G et on the lift, Jake," Raynor demanded. He was in no mood for Jake's antics. All he wanted to do was deliver the cargo, quickly catch up with an old friend and then leave. He never felt comfortable at social events. Lots of people in one place agitated him.

"No! Why can't I stay on *Galaxy*?" Jake pleaded.

"You're never going to learn anything by just staying on the ship. You need to be more involved."

"I can't. I'm scared."

"Don't make me force you," Raynor said. "Because I will drag you, kicking and screaming if I have to. I don't care."

Jake looked at Rob and Diputs for help, but they just rolled their eyes and turned away from him. He continued to plead with Raynor. "Why do I have to go?"

"We have goods to deliver and it's your role to deliver goods."

"Then why is everyone else going?"

"Are you kidding?" Persephone exclaimed. "All sorts of people are going to be there. It's a terrific opportunity to get dressed up and mingle."

"And stuff your face," Diputs said gleefully.

"I was actually invited," Rob added.

"What are you so afraid of, Jake?" Persephone asked gently. "It's just a lift."

"This thing doesn't even have walls! It's just a flying disc with handrails! What if I fall off? I just can't do it. Isn't there some other way to get up there?"

Raynor looked past the towering buildings surrounding them and up to their destination; the very top of the space station. The only thing connecting it to the city was a vast shell to keep the atmosphere inside.

"To be honest, I'd be more worried about someone throwing you off," Raynor said. "And this is the only way up."

Jake didn't answer, no doubt unsure how to take the idle threat.

Raynor's Link chimed. He held the terminal out in front of him, an image floated above it. The incoming communication was from an unknown source and appeared to be encrypted. He held up his Link and glanced at the others. "I'll be back in a moment. Can someone make sure Jake gets on this damn lift before I get back? Diputs, with me."

They headed down the enormous platform of the laser lift docks to find a quiet place to talk privately. When they were clear of the others, Raynor tapped on his Link to accept the connection. "Cliff, how are things?"

"Are you in a secure location?" Cliff asked. He sounded panicked. Which was unusual for him.

"Not really. We're on *M1*. But this is an encrypted Link, and no one's in earshot, besides Diputs. What's the matter?"

"They threatened to kill me..."

"Who did?" Diputs asked and exchanged a worried look with Raynor.

"The mutants," Raynor guessed.

"You don't think they could get me on Mars, could they?"

"Of course not," Diputs reassured him.

"It's us they'll come after," Raynor added. "They may well be waiting for us the next time we venture close to the asteroid belt or deep space. It seems like the safest thing we can do right now is to stay put."

"I think they may have people on the inside," Cliff said. "Working within the Colonies."

"Anything's possible," Raynor grumbled. "A human working for the mutants isn't half as dangerous as the mutants themselves. I'm not worried about any assailants the mutants send our way."

"*I'm* worried about it!" Cliff insisted. "And what if they send a small army? What then?"

Raynor shook his head. "Don't be ridiculous. Where do you think they would get those kinds of resources?"

"We just gave them the resources! What do you think those blueprints were? It was basically the formula to turn more of *us* into more of *them*. Listen, just watch your back, Raynor. I like having someone I can rely on to be discreet."

Diputs smiled awkwardly at Cliff through the Link.

"And, you too, umm..."

"Diputs."

"Whatever."

The connection ended and Raynor's Link turned back into a blank transparent panel.

"I'd say we are pretty safe for the moment," Raynor said. "Security should be ramped up here due to the Anamnesis. This should be the safest station in the Colonies right now."

"Guess we can have some free time while we're here," Diputs agreed. "But we can't exactly stay forever."

They made their way back to the laser lifts where they found the rest of the crew waiting patiently on the platform.

"Look at you, Jake," Diputs said with a laugh. " Facing your fears like a man. What changed your mind?"

"It turns out I am more afraid of Persephone," Jake said timidly.

Persephone smirked, beaming with satisfaction.

"Good work, Seph," Raynor said. "Now, let's get on our way, shall we?"

Rob activated the laser lift from a small control interface on the handrail and the platform hummed upwards. Raynor watched Jake cling to the railing as they launched into the air and accelerated up towards the observation decks. The wind whipped at their faces and flung their hair in all directions. They had to raise their voices to hear each other.

"What do you think happened to Lisa?" Rob asked. "I haven't seen her since we docked. I was absolutely sure she would be busy *observing* us right now."

"Miss your girlfriend, Rob?" Raynor joked.

"No!" Rob said with a disapproving scowl.

"Actually, I think she went up ahead of us," Persephone said. "Probably reporting on us to Swift."

"Well, that's going to be one boring report," Raynor shouted. "If she had anything on us at all, she would have used it by now.

"She's kept busy so far going through the vast amounts of data in the ship's logs," Rob said, his words only just audible. "We must be careful though. We don't know what she is really up to."

Raynor raised an eyebrow. "What do you mean?"

"Have you considered what Lisa was placed to observe us doing exactly?

"Spy on us for Swift?"

"Well, yes," Rob agreed. "But I think there's more. Just as we are given this Artifact to deliver, it gets stolen by outlaws, and somehow, we can go on like nothing even happened? It's very strange. It's all a little too coincidental for my liking. What if our superiors know that we actually still have it?"

"Then why haven't they done anything about it?" Diputs asked. "You sound paranoid. Well, more so than usual. It's pretty obvious that the reason for her being on *Galaxy* is because of Reen."

Rob scowled. "No, that was the reason she was placed on board initially. The reason she remains on board is still suspicious. Look, the bottom line is if she catches on to any of our operations, then we're all in trouble."

Raynor looked over the railing at the spectacular city below. He knew all too well how much was at stake. He felt the laser lift slow down as it approached the observation decks. It fit perfectly into a circular junction in the docking terminal. Inside, everything was made of rare materials; scarce types of wood and fabric with brass fixtures to induce a feeling of warmth and luxury. Jake breathed a loud sigh of relief as they stepped off the lift. Persephone pulled her Link out from her simple black dress and tapped away at it.

The dress exploded into a magnificent green gown that looked like it was made of a million feathers.

"Well?" Persephone said, turning slightly to give Raynor a better view. "What do you think? Do you like it?"

"I'm glad I don't have to dress up like that."

"Yeah, I can see that! You could have worn something nicer than your standard-issue work attire."

"Why? I *am* working." Raynor looked at a map on his Link and followed a ramp that spiralled up, leading them deeper into the observation decks. The first few levels were dark, quiet, and empty of people.

Diputs frowned. "Where's the party?"

"It's this way," Raynor said. "Now remember, you lot aren't really meant to be here, so try to go with the flow and don't draw attention to yourselves. We might have convinced the security protocols to let you on the lift, but there will be actual people up here watching over things. Keep your eyes and ears open. You might learn something useful."

"I'm *actually* meant to be here," Rob reminded them.

"We know," they all said in unison.

Raynor led the way up the ramp to the next level. He stopped suddenly at the top, frozen at the sight of the crowd. He glanced around at all the people dressed in formal attire who were chatting, laughing, and sipping clear liquid from fine crystal. He scanned the room for potential threats or anything that seemed out of the ordinary. The entire area was surrounded by Enforcers, which should have put him at ease. He had to remind himself several times that these people were the elite of Colony representatives.

"Parasites," Diputs grumbled. "Living off the labour of hard-working colonists."

"They keep the air fresh and the Organix in good supply," Raynor said. "They've probably earned this."

"Are you okay?" Persephone touched his shoulder.

"I'm fine. I need to find a man named Jackson Bainsby. Just stay close and try not to get lost."

The others seemed to be getting restless. Rob pushed his chest out and straightened his coat. "Well, I'm going to mingle with the science community."

"Try not to agitate the Jaren diplomats this time," Raynor said. "They made it quite hard for us to get landing authorisation on our last visit after you accused them of misappropriating your research."

"They did!" Rob grumbled.

"Well, you didn't have to head-butt the chairman of the Europa Technology Institute!"

"He was a stupid creet who deserved it. Don't worry about me, I'll Link you if I happen to get in any trouble." Rob walked away, leaving them to their task.

Raynor began his search for Bainsby with Diputs, Persephone and Jake in pursuit. They weaved in and out of pressed uniforms and holo-dresses, stopping to eavesdrop on the occasional bit of intriguing conversation or chatter.

Eventually, he spotted Bainsby, his old professor, lavishing attention on several young ladies. It had been some time since

Raynor had last seen the Historian, and he hadn't aged a bit. His rough appearance and scars stood out in contrast with his fine clothes and surroundings. Raynor had always admired him for his sense of adventure and defiant ideals.

"The homeworld?" Bainsby grimaced. "A victim of faith, reinforced by zealotry, stoked by hatred and armed with a thousand generations of human military advancement. Not even a planet can stand up to that."

Raynor had heard the rant a million times, he questioned exactly how much the story had been embellished and wasn't ready to just accept it at face value.

Bainsby looked up at Raynor as he emerged from the crowd. "Raynor Spartin. It's good to see you again, I wasn't expecting you to arrive so soon! Did you get the item I asked for?"

Raynor nodded and pulled a cylindrical white canister from his pocket.

"Aha! I have been looking forward to this," Bainsby said, grasping the tiny object.

"It was exactly where you said it would be. How do you even know about this, anyway? The Terranean Expanse is supposed to be off limits."

"Keep your voice down," Bainsby whispered. "You know how much trouble we would be in if anyone knew I sent you there?"

"Well, what is it then?" Raynor asked in a hushed voice. "What's inside that cylinder that's so valuable that you would have us risk our arses to get it for you?"

"You've seen it, it's a gold coin. People used to be measured by how many of these they possessed before the Value system was in place."

"I know what a coin is, but there are probably billions of them floating around out there. What makes this one so important?"

Bainsby glanced around suspiciously. "We should take this discussion to my private athenaeum."

Raynor turned back to his companions. "I need to speak to Bainsby in private. You can either go back to the ship or wait for me here. It's up to you."

"But I thought I was meant to be learning," Jake said, sounding disappointed.

"Lesson over," Raynor said. "Go and enjoy yourself."

Without further delay, he followed Bainsby away from the crowd. They walked in silence until they had passed out of the congregation areas and into the winding corridors of the upper levels.

"Raynor, I'm curious. When you agreed to take on this little expedition for me, what were you expecting in return?"

Raynor grinned. "I want information."

DATAFILE

Unity

NODE 1

A Unity is a formal partnership between two or more people to merge their Value. There are very few restrictions regarding who can form a unity. Anyone or any number of people, who have completed adolescence, and are freely willing may enter a legally binding unity so long as everyone involved is in agreement. People can also join a unity after it has been formed under the same conditions.

NODE 2

There are three primary reasons that individuals enter or form a unity:

1. Combined living allocations and shared resources

2. Procreation

3. Forma diplomatic alliances

Once in a unity, individual Value is no longer recognised. Instead, the Value is assessed by the unity (as a whole). This means in most cases the Unity Value (UV) will be the same as its highest Valued individual. However, the forming of a unity by key individuals can be beneficial for the Colonies. In those cases, the benefiting Colonies grant a higher UV to the unity than any of the individuals would normally be able to attain on their own.

NODE 3

Under certain circumstances, one or more individuals may choose to leave a unity (Dissociation). These include irreconcilable differences, social dysfunction (physical or emotional), or when a predetermined goal or outcome has been reached.

CHAPTER FOUR

Out of Place

Diputs watched Raynor walk away from the lounge with the weird old man. He felt his stomach grumbling, which reminded him of his real objective. He had been on Organix for so long that just the thought of a slow roasted leg of meat made him salivate. It had been almost a whole cycle since he had last eaten anything real. Sure, Organix provided a practical and comprehensive source of sustenance while out in space, but it didn't really satisfy the hunger.

"Are you sure they are going to serve real food here?" Jake asked eagerly. "You said they would be."

"Of course they will, spazmoid. Do you really think they would serve Organix for the colony elite?" Diputs asked.

He looked around at the crowds of nicely dressed delegates. Lots of people gawked out of the large viewing portals which looked over the thousands of chunks of rock and debris that were the remains of the homeworld.

He noticed robotoids flying above everyone's heads, scanning the area below, looking for whoever required their assistance. It was like watching a floating train of food and drink. One would drop down out of its place in the line when someone raised their hand to signal for it. There was exotic food from all over the Colonies—fruits, vegetables, and even simulated protein. They were all paired up and then wrapped together and cut into bite-sized pieces. The smells were overwhelming.

"Hey, you!" Diputs shouted. "Floating drink platform, come over here!"

The shiny silver robot manoeuvred silently towards him and hovered in place, waiting for him to take something. He took a glass of clear liquid from the tray, examined it and took a sip. His nose puckered, and he dropped the glass back on the tray. "Yuck, Synthohol! Permitted alcohol is just the worst."

He smiled at Jake and Persephone, then motioned to another of the flying robotoids. It hovered down to chest height. This one was much better; tiny cubes of beef, glazed with the slightest hint of gravy on top of beetroot and some sort of green leaf with a sweet potato base. He started grabbing food and stuffing it into his mouth. Persephone looked at Jake. The two of them shrugged and joined in.

Jake stopped a platter of what appeared to be small medical discs in a variety of colours. "Why does this one have med-discs on it? They aren't food."

Diputs paused between mouthfuls to gaze pityingly at his crewmate. "Really, Jake? Really?"

"No way! Simules!" Persephone exclaimed. "These discs chemically replicate real emotions. You can't just get these at any party." She grabbed one and placed it on her exposed shoulder. The blue disc dissolved into her skin. "This one is excitement!"

"Doesn't sound like you need it," Diputs smirked.

Jake looked at her sceptically.

"Try one," she said, insistently holding out a light blue disc.

"No thanks. I am fine with my own emotions."

Persephone shrugged and placed it on her other shoulder. She quickly stiffened and let out a short high-pitched squeal before covering her mouth with one hand. "Oh my gosh!"

Jake's eyes widened. "What is it? Are you alright?"

"Oh, wow!" Persephone gasped and clenched her dress as if she were trying to pull it off. She squeezed her legs together and leant on Jake to keep herself upright. Jake looked horrified and Diputs could only laugh when he saw the confusion twitch across the boy's face.

"Do you want me to get help?" Jake asked.

"No, Jake! Fuck!" Persephone moaned.

Now all the guests around them were watching, enjoying the show. The public display even drew the attention of some Enforcers, who grinned and nudged each other in jest. Persephone didn't seem to care. She collapsed to her knees and let out one last moan as her entire body shuddered. Some people clapped and laughed as though it was entirely put on for their amusement, then they all went back to their conversations like nothing had happened.

"Wow, that must have been some powerful emotion," Jake said.

"I umm, have to go," she exclaimed and turned to hurry away from them.

"Wait, where are you going?"

"Shut up Jake. I need to freshen up." Persephone hobbled away like she had just wet herself.

Diputs picked up several drumsticks and ripped the chicken flesh off them, swallowing it hungrily. He was making such a show of eating that other guests started looking at him with disgust. Even though he was wearing his fine clothes, his coat still bore the Operator emblem on it for all to see.

"What is a ship's Operator doing here?" A lady nearby asked him suspiciously. "You would hardly have enough Value for an invite."

Diputs gazed at her with a mouth full of food and a look of puzzlement. He finished chewing and swallowed. "I'm accompanying an invited guest, what about it?"

"Well, you don't really look like you belong here."

Diputs thought for a moment, he looked around the room for something, anything he might be able to use to take the attention away from him. He exchanged a look with a steward who was standing nearby watching the goings-on. He looked even more out of place than Diputs.

"What about that guy?" Diputs said, pointing out the steward. Diputs looked closer, interested to see how he would react. "Just look at him, he hasn't shaved in rotations, messy hair, not at all like the other well-groomed people here."

The steward looked uncomfortable with Diputs' statement and tried to back away from the situation. Diputs took a few steps forward and grabbed the steward's wrist. Instantly he noticed the tattoo on the man's forearm. Many people had tattoos, but Diputs had seen this design before.

"That is an interesting tattoo," he said, pulling the steward's sleeve up further. "Where did you get it?"

The steward instinctively tugged at his sleeve to cover his marking, but Diputs had already seen enough. The tattoo was a sun shining rays of light in all directions. Diputs recalled where he had seen that symbol before. His old guardian, Barron Addler, had one almost identical. Something that had linked him to a shady and mysterious past and kept him from a life in the Colonies. As a result, Diputs had no idea if the man was even still alive.

If something suspicious was going on here, exposing the steward now could result in great danger to himself and all the people around him. He watched as the attention he was placing on the man made him start to panic. "That's a symbol from the solar fields on Lunar, isn't it?" Diputs lied, hoping the man would realise he was steering the conversation in a less threatening direction.

The steward visibly relaxed, though his eyes were wary. "Yes, sir. You are correct."

"So, what brings a solar harvester to a place like this?"

The background buzz of conversation resumed as spectators turned away.

"I don't mean to be rude, sir, but I am needed elsewhere," he excused himself feebly.

Diputs watched the man hurry off. He turned back to Jake, who was still stuffing his face. "I'm going to follow him."

"Suit yourself," Jake answered through a mouth full of bread. "I'm staying here. This is amazing!"

Diputs laughed mockingly. "No, you're not. Now follow me."

"But what about the food? And Persephone?"

"Now, Jake! We can catch up with Persephone and the others later."

Jake lowered his head in defeat and followed Diputs.

Diputs ran after the Steward. "Quickly he went this way."

They threaded through the crowd and came to an elevator. They stepped onto the platform that whizzed downward to the lower observation decks. They jumped out of the elevator and looked around cautiously. The lower decks seemed to be devoid of people.

"Are you sure he went this way?" Jake asked.

Diputs looked around. "Pretty sure. Be quiet and listen."

"What is all this stuff?" Jake asked, gesturing to the large museum halls around them. It was littered with old pieces of technology and art preserved through time.

"You really have been living under a rock, haven't you! How do you not know about any of this?"

"I don't know, I just—"

"It doesn't matter," Diputs said sharply. "We need to find where the Steward went!"

"Why?"

"I've seen it before, that tattoo he had of the Divine Sun, I want to find out what it means. I also think he may be up to no good."

"Why didn't you mention that when we were surrounded by Enforcers?" Jake asked. "They would have sorted it out real easy."

"I wanted to make sure before I acted. Who knows what he might have done if I called the Enforcers? He could have taken a hostage and started killing people. Best case scenario is they would have taken us all away for questioning. Meanwhile, there could be more of them executing some deadly plan, with us powerless to stop them," Diputs explained.

Jake crossed his arms. "Are you listening to yourself? *You* sound paranoid!"

Suddenly Diputs' ears pricked up at the sound of footsteps coming from behind them. "Shhh. Do you hear that?"

Diputs turned, in time for a figure to appear around the corner of a large relic at a dead run. Jake yelped as the collision knocked Diputs sprawling. He looked up into the face of a tall dark-haired woman, staring at him in indignation.

"Watch where you are going!" she snapped at him but stooped down to help him up anyway. When she saw who he was, her whole demeanour changed. "Toney?! What are you doing here?" the woman asked with genuine surprise.

"Serena?" He stared up at a face he thought he would never see again. "What? Why are you here?"

"I'm working," she said and looked away from his gaze.

An awkward silence ensued. Seeing Serena again brought up painful memories for Diputs that he thought he had long buried. She had split up with him, right before he took the Operator role on Galaxy, and this was the first time he had seen or even spoken to her since. He was flooded with emotions that pulled him in every direction. He didn't know which way was up. Her voice snapped him out of his train of thought.

"Are you staying long?" she asked.

"Probably not."

"What do you mean *probably*?" Serena stepped closer to him and whispered in his ear. "Toney, I know you have no reason to listen to me, but you must leave the station immediately! Just go, right now. Get off *M1*!"

Diputs' eyes widened with surprise.

A voice echoed through the nearby corridor. "Glitch! Hurry up. We need to go!"

"Glitch? Is that the name you are going by now?" Diputs snapped.

"Just come with me," she pleaded. "I'll explain all of this later." She placed her hand on Diputs' arm and he jerked backwards.

"Look, I, I think you should go," Diputs replied.

"Glitch!" the voice shouted again.

Serena looked desperate. She caught Diputs' eye one last time then she turned around and fled. Diputs was dumbfounded. He looked to Jake, but the gaze the boy returned showed only confusion. So, he pulled out his Link and tried to contact Raynor. A message flashed across the display.

'CONNECTION LOST'

"Saturn's balls! I think it's already begun!"

"Aww, are we missing the Anamnesis?" Jake asked.

"No, you idiot, they are jamming all communications. I need you to go and find the others right away! Go and tell Raynor!"

"Umm... what do you want me to tell Raynor?" Jake asked, still waiting for instruction.

"Tell him to meet me at the laser lift docks, I may need his help."

"But why? What exactly do you think is going on here?"

Diputs rubbed his temples. "That steward had a strange tattoo. I think it may be an obscure reference to the outlaws. You know, the same people who kidnapped you and tortured Raynor to death?"

"Then why don't we report this to the Enforcers? Let them deal with it! That's their role."

Diputs looked at Jake like he had three heads. "We don't even know why they are here! Serena warned me to get off the station. I'm not sure if that's because she doesn't want me to get in her way, or because they are planning something bigger than a kidnapping this time. If we go to the Enforcers, talking about an outlaw attack, they will most likely just lock us up," he said sternly. But the boy only looked back at him sceptically.

"You don't know that," Jake mumbled in response.

"I am the Senior Technical Operator, you're just a ship hand," Diputs snapped. "That means I get to tell you what to do. I need to follow her and find out more. Just go and tell Raynor that there are outlaws on the station. If things start to go bad, then get everyone to evacuate."

That silenced Jake's protests. He nodded and turned back the way they came, leaving Diputs to pursue Serena.

It didn't take long for Diputs to catch up with her and the Steward. They were engrossed in an argument which was slowing them down. They had stopped in front of the laser lifts and were calling up all the platforms. Diputs stood behind a corner and watched as they unpacked and assembled some electronic devices.

"I just don't get it. What the fuck happened back there with that colonist creet?" the steward asked Serena as they attached one of the devices to the first lift. "Why would you associate yourself with that scum?"

"Don't forget I used to be a colonist too," she breathed out softly. "And that creet was my ex."

"Get your head back in the game. This is more important than who you used to lay down for. You should have killed him," he said. Scolding her while fitting the next device.

"I know, Scrub. But—"

"But nothing. You knew what this was. People were always going to die. If he suspected anything, he could be bringing the Enforcers here as we speak."

Those words confirmed Diputs' worst fears. They were here to kill people. He spotted a blaster sitting unattended with the rest of their gear and equipment. He watched to make sure that they weren't looking in his direction.

"Anyway, if he meant so much to you then why did you leave each other in the first place?" Scrub asked.

"I left him," Serena said. "We just weren't going in the same direction, so he went his own way."

"You could have come with me," Diputs whispered to himself.

"That's fucking great," Scrub answered Serena. "Let's hope we get these attached before he brings an army down on us. Hand me the last one so we can finish this and get out of here."

Diputs had to act now. He leapt out of his cover, scooped up the blaster and pointed it at the outlaws.

"I want you to stop right there and put down the device," he instructed carefully. They both looked up at him in surprise.

Serena looked at Scrub, his hands were raised over his head and the device was armed at his feet. Scrub began to step off the platform.

"Wait! Don't move," Diputs said.

Scrub still had one foot on the platform and the other on the laser lift.

"What have you done?" Diputs demanded.

"You wouldn't understand," Serena insisted. "You just—"

"We will not be slaves to the Colonies!" Scrub shouted. "We are following the Divine Will!"

"No, you're not!" Diputs said with disgust. "Serena, you need to listen to me. You need to take those things off the laser lifts and deactivate them."

"Oh, I don't think so," Scrub chided. He smiled at Diputs and lifted his foot.

All three laser lifts shot out from the dock and descended at once towards the city. Air rushed out as the lifts ejected and Scrub waved his arms to keep his balance. He almost fell into the gap that was left by the circular platforms.

"Make them stop!" Diputs yelled. He tightened his grip on the blaster, reminding them that he was ready to shoot.

The area shuddered with the impact of the explosion from the laser lift platforms. Diputs stepped cautiously to the hole, looked down through the gap and saw a giant red fireball erupting. This afforded Scrub the opportunity to tackle Diputs to the ground. They grappled and struggled against each other. With ease, Scrub knocked the weapon from Diputs' grasp and belted him in the face with a closed fist. Diputs raised his arms trying to deflect the blows. Scrub dived over, scooped up the blaster and then rolled to his feet. He took aim at Diputs.

"STOP!" Serena screamed.

CHAPTER FIVE

Intrigue

The door dematerialised and Raynor followed Bainsby into the athenaeum. The spacious area was decorated with exquisite artwork. Like most of the other locations, the far wall was lined with viewing portals looking out into the depths of space. Ancient relics sat on plinths placed strategically around the dwelling.

Raynor found himself drawn to a painting of a ship with white sails in a rough ocean battling a fierce storm. He touched the edge of the painting and the whole room was suddenly engulfed with ferocious waves. While the ground stayed firmly under his feet, he could feel the spray of saltwater on his face and the chill of the wind blowing through him. He could hear distant shouts from the crew of the sailing ship as an enormous wave crashed into it sending one man overboard. He let go of the painting and the room returned to normal. Not a drop of water to be seen.

Bainsby stood behind a workstation and looked up patiently from the interface. He gave no notice to what had just happened. "By the sounds of things, we are after the same information," he said. "How does someone in your position come to know about the Artifact?"

"What do you mean?" Raynor asked. "How is that even possible? Are you saying these two things are somehow related?"

Raynor didn't know what to think. He felt a slight warmth emanating from the Artifact in his jacket pocket. It was a supporting comfort which left him feeling stronger and more alert. He was starting to realise that he was glad to have come across the Artifact, despite the hardships he had gone through to acquire it. He was fascinated by it. He needed to know where it had come from and what it was doing. He could feel its effects, but he wanted to know everything it was capable of.

"Oh, come on. Don't be sketchy," Bainsby said, snapping him back into the conversation. "Almost no one even knows of its existence. And yet, somehow, you've actually been in contact with it? I know you couldn't have just stumbled across it in one of your shady deals. This is much bigger than you can imagine."

"Actually, no. We were assigned to transfer it from Mars to a remote facility."

"Ah! I knew it! Mars had it all along. I knew they must have been protecting something. Why else would they have the most superior military of all the Colonies?"

"Protecting it? From what?"

Bainsby ignored Raynor's question. "What really happened to it? Where exactly were you supposed to be taking it?"

"We were taking it to a research facility when outlaws attacked us. They stole it, but then Swift destroyed their vessel and it was lost in the explosion," Raynor explained.

Bainsby narrowed his eyes. "I highly doubt that."

"Why do you doubt it? It's pretty much Swift's fault."

"I highly doubt that as well. The Artifact can't be destroyed that easily. And Swift, well, it seems he must be after it as well"

Bainsby raised the white canister up and twisted it. There was a snap and a hiss as vapour shot out, dissipating quickly. He pulled the two half cylinders apart to reveal the contents. Light gleamed from the small golden coin. It was rough, with tiny dents all over and chunks taken out of it. He slipped it into the interface in the middle of the chamber and a holographic slide appeared above.

Raynor crossed the room to get a closer look. "Is that an audio file?" he asked, pointing at a symbol of a curved line in a rectangular box.

Bainsby nodded. "You see, back then, agents who protected these secrets would encode files into the ridges of coins as a way to communicate undetected."

He played the file:

"We have secured the Ark," the first voice stated.

"Very good. We don't have much time left. They have broken through barrier eight," the second voice said. The conversation skipped.

"We can't be thinking about actually using this, can we? This is madness," the first voice said.

"We have no choice! All is lost. This is the only way."

The dialogue was corrupted and hard to make out. It seemed like only part of a longer conversation.

"What is this?" Raynor questioned, desperately trying to put things together in his mind.

Bainsby stopped the recording. "It goes on for a while. Proof that the Artifact is part of a mighty weapon. Whoever these people were, they had access to a weapon so powerful that it destroyed the homeworld," he said in awe.

Bainsby took the coin off the holo and replaced it with a data crystal. A holographic image of the Artifact appeared.

"That's it!" Raynor confirmed.

"Aha! So you opened it, too!" Bainsby grinned, giving Raynor a knowing look.

"Well, yes, but—"

"As you can see it appears to be fractured and broken off from something larger," Bainsby explained. "The colonies have no idea what it is, where it's from, or what it does. I had no idea who had it until now."

"And who's that?" Raynor asked nervously.

"Well, I can only assume Swift has it from what you've told me. He would have scoured the debris of that outlaw ship until he found it."

Raynor nodded as if to confirm Bainsby's suspicions.

"So, you see, we are both after the same thing, my friend. I have been searching for information on this for many cycles."

"In the recording, they referred to an Ark. What does that mean?"

"From what I have been able to decipher in these old texts, it roughly means: *vessel of immense power*."

"If it's just a small part of some weapon of mass destruction, what happened to the rest of it? And why do you want it?"

There was a loud rumble that shook the room. The lights flickered and Raynor grabbed hold of the bench to steady himself. "What was that?"

"No, not now! Not during the Anamnesis! This stupid station has issue after issue."

An alarm sounded and several warnings appeared on the interface. The words 'CRITICAL' and 'DANGER' flashed in red and Bainsby pressed at the alerts frantically, trying to resolve the issues.

"Control, what is going on?" Bainsby asked.

No one answered. A bead of sweat rolled down his face. He looked at Raynor briefly, then stormed out of his office and ran down the corridor. Raynor took off in pursuit. Bainsby appeared to be heading directly to the emergency exit.

"What are you doing?" Raynor shouted at him.

Bainsby didn't answer but Raynor had already caught him. They both crashed to the ground as Raynor tackled his old professor.

"Get off me you fool. We need to get off this bloody death trap."

There was a loud hiss of rushing air. They both looked up to see the escape pods floating away.

Bainsby stood up and brushed himself off. "Well then, we had better go to the event hall and tell everyone what has happened."

"And what is that exactly?"

Bainsby frowned. "Isn't it obvious? The station is falling apart. We should get everyone to evacuate."

Raynor wasn't entirely convinced. His instincts told him that something wasn't right with Bainsby, who was now casually walking down the corridor. Raynor decided to stay close behind to see what the Historian was really up to.

ORGANIX
MADE FOR YOU
INTRODUCING
GREEN...
NEW FORMULA GIVES YOU MORE FOCUS AND ENERGY! MEETS ALL OF YOUR ESSENTIAL DAILY SUSTENANCE NEEDS. NOW IN YOUR ORGANIX DISPENSER!
TASTES... AMAZING!
Made and distributed by the Lunar Colony | Maximum of 3 units per day | For all Values

CHAPTER SIX

Objective

Clarissa couldn't believe what she was seeing. She stared in anguish at the hundreds of escape pods as they slowly drifted away. Silence fell over the crowd as it became apparent that something out of the ordinary was going on. Slowly a low mumble of questions escalated into panic. People started to scream and push as realisation set in that the only way to get off the station was to use one of three tiny platforms to get back to Aurora city and onto a ship. Clarissa heard a message coming through the internal Emergency Broadcast System, but she could not understand it over the noise.

"Quiet!" Peacekeeper Dalton's voice bellowed. It seemed to work. Everyone in the Event Hall stopped and turned to him. Her father climbed onto a table. "Let's not lose our heads here, people. There is no evidence of an *attack*. Just let me Link to the control centre and see what is going on. I'm sure it's just a minor malfunction."

"Someone's blocking the signal! We can't communicate with anyone," someone called out frantically.

"It's those krankers!" one man yelled, igniting a flurry of outrage from the Saturn Alliance representatives. "They've never been trustworthy."

"That's enough!" Dalton insisted. "I would like all delegates to split up into your Colonies and keep your people safe while we find the underlying cause of this. I want the Enforcers to do a sweep of the station, check all rooms and corridors."

"So you can round us all up for the slaughter?" a woman called out from the restless crowd.

"Spoken like a true dirter," a nearby Jaren said. "I'm sure you're not above sacrificing some of your own to kill off a few of us."

"I've been a Peacekeeper for longer than you've been alive, Sarco. My fairness and integrity won't be challenged by the same Jaren who had to be bailed out after smuggling chronium from the Saturn Alliance. The creation of the Nexus Treaty is one of the most important things that separates us from the savage outlaws! We need to confirm what the threat is, so we can respond in kind and begin to evacuate the observation decks in an orderly manner. If the situation requires it."

"So where are all the Martians then?" another Jaren called out.

"Yeah, and where is Swift? It's a bit suspicious that he is conveniently missing from this gathering," someone else said.

"Where are any of the high-up Martian representatives?" another voice shouted. Others echoed this opinion.

Clarissa watched the crowds of people turning on the Martians. Some were physically attacked and restrained while others stood their ground and fought back. She couldn't believe how quickly they all turned to violence when nothing had even been established yet. "Stop it!" She screamed. "Can't you all hear yourselves? We have been at peace for such a brief time, why are you all so determined to destroy it? Has it even occurred to anyone that this could all be an accident, technological malfunction, or just human error? Why is everything so black and white with you people?"

"I'm not sitting back to be killed at the hands of those dirt-hoarding Martians," someone in the crowd shouted.

The pushing and shoving grew worse and Clarissa was knocked to the ground. She put one hand on her throbbing head, looked up and saw a ripple of air distort the wall behind it. The distortion took the form of a silver mech suit. It phased into full view and stood towering over her. The large figure reached down to scoop her up, lifting her gently to her feet.

Everyone around her stepped back, surprised by the intrusion of this metal warrior. The helmet and visor retracted to reveal Supreme Commander Swift. Clarissa's heart raced at the sight of the Martian Commander in his battle-ready armour. She realised he must have been standing there for some time watching and listening to everything that had unfolded.

"You bunch of useless creets. This isn't a Martian attack," Swift's voice crashed over them. "You spend your precious hours pontificating on the minutiae of colonial life as if it matters, completely blind to the fact that we have all been gathered here like animals to surrender to the brute force of the UAE. I've been out there, I've seen it. There is no haven to escape to. Only abysmal fucking cold!"

"You can't pass the blame that easily," Eryn piped up. "You do realise that you just admitted that you have been spying on us all this whole time? How can we be sure that we can trust you, Ryan?"

"How about you shut the fuck up, Eryn," Swift suggested bitterly. "I have seen more action than the lot of you combined. I have stopped actual threats to Mars on more occasions than this snivelling little punk has had intellectual thoughts."

"Excuse me! I'll have you know I'm about to be the Supreme Commander of the new UAE fleet. Your troops will be reporting to me soon."

Swift gritted his teeth and looked at Eryn with a gaze that could have melted tectanium.

Eryn's pompous voice and arrogant tone immediately agitated Clarissa, so she decided to speak up. "Are you saying there is no actual outlaw threat, Swift?"

"Of course I'm not saying that," Swift admitted. "All I'm saying is that the Nexus is using the outlaw threat as an excuse to create a fleet larger than anyone else. Sure, they might crush the outlaws. Then what? None of us would be able to stand on our own without fear of being suppressed by the UAE. The Peacekeepers know how fragile things are between colonies at the moment. You lot have proven that right here by how quickly you all fell apart and turned on each other. They want peace alright, and they will enforce it with an iron fist. This whole thing is probably a setup to scare us into submission."

"Do you understand how insane you sound?" Dalton shouted back.

"Well, obviously I don't expect you to throw your full support behind my opinion, Dalton. You know, if you weren't such a puppet, I would think this whole thing was your idea."

"What exactly are you trying to achieve here?" A gruff voice queried. It was Arrol Jaines coming to Dalton's defence. "Do you really think making wild accusations about the UAE will make this situation better? Or are you trying to take people's minds off the fact that you, perhaps, are responsible for trapping us all here on the observation decks? That's right. While you've all been bickering, none of you have noticed that the laser lifts, our only way down to Aurora, have been destroyed."

Swift looked genuinely shocked by the news, but he kept his composure well. "I'll tell you what I am doing. I am getting to the bottom of this nonsense right now! I'm going to the control centre to get some answers. Like why haven't we heard a single thing from any of the station staff since the escape pods misfired? Just look at the stewards all standing around like the rest of you mindless drones. Come on, how about you do something constructive other than stuffing your faces and assaulting each other?"

"I should probably go with you," a small voice struggled to be heard over the crowd.

Everyone looked around to see who it was. The crowd slowly parted for a short, round, pig-faced scientist as he made his way through to Swift.

"Robert Crane," Swift muttered.

Clarissa had heard of him before. He was supposedly one of the Martians' most revered scientists.

"Fine, you can come. Who else? Lisa? Where's my Observer?" Swift called.

Clarissa looked around to where she had seen the cyborg moments before. She was no longer there. Clarissa again felt a deep pang of sorrow for the woman. She must have been disheartened to think Swift might have been listening to their earlier conversation about him.

"Take me!" a fiery redhead spoke out from the crowd. "You could use some muscle. You know, just in case."

"Alright, Persephone, you can come," Swift agreed.

"I'll go too," Peacekeeper Dalton added.

"No. I'll go," Clarissa insisted confidently. Her father looked surprised by her initiative.

"You should stay here and try to keep some sort of order," she said. "You do want me to be more involved, don't you?"

Dalton hesitated, then gave her a nod of approval and the group set off for the control centre.

DATAFILE

The Value System

NODE 1

The Value System is a resource-based economy to ensure that everyone is recognised for their contribution to society. In exchange for their allegiance, each colonist is assigned a Value Rating that reflects their level of contribution and importance. Value is not a unit or number that can be traded, spent, or accumulated. It instead acts as an indicator of what benefits a person is entitled to.

All essential goods and services are unlimited to anyone who wants or needs them. Colonists are all assigned a role, in which they work to make themselves valuable to their colony, rather than exchanging their goods and services or time for items of perceived equal value. Roles are assigned by the colonies based on need and suitability but can also be exchanged for another role of choice under certain circumstances.

NODE 2

The function of the Value system is to distribute resources to the population based on their contribution to society and to reward people who excel/contribute more than others. Various levels of Value are allocated to give a clear advantage to people who contribute more by possessing the required skills or taking greater risks than others. If any person refuses to contribute by neglecting their assigned role without good reason, the colony will cease to allow them access to any living essentials, protection, or resources.

NODE 3

The Value system was created by the pioneering colonies—Lunar and Mars—when a lack of resources meant that they needed to break free of the old economical restraints and institute a new system whereby the colonies could issue resources based on who was considered to be essential in sustaining the growth of their new society. Since the colonies are now in a state of plenty, resources are provided in three categories: Essential, Required and Rated.

CHAPTER SEVEN

Aurora

Lazarus felt as if he was suspended in mid-air. Transparent panels atop the bustling Transway of Aurora's central district elevated them above carriages, whizzing beneath their feet, shooting by at incredible speeds. They moved in perfect unison with each other, all being coordinated by Nexus. He looked back at Appel who was trailing behind him. Towering buildings reached up high all around, backed by the light teal sky which gave the city of Aurora a surreal ambience. Citizens walked around the district going about their business. The silver and white colours of the Lunar Colony were the most common, worn by the people who lived and worked on *M1*.

He had grown up in Aurora. The unity his parents had created only cultivated low Value, but that didn't stop him from enjoying his childhood. He was used to getting by with only the bare essentials. What use were objects if you lived in a six by twelve metron apartment? There were only so many possessions one could keep in such a limited space. Regardless, this city had remained his favourite place in Sol. Now he was older, and had travelled the rest of the system in his role as an Operator Shiphand on *Galaxy*. but he always loved coming back to his home. He felt a spring in his step as he walked along the thoroughfare.

Appel smiled at him. "I don't think I've ever seen you this excited."

"What's not to be excited about? I'm back home! And I'm thinking about getting one of those Synchronous implants. Then I would always be able to connect to the collective. No more having to carry a Link everywhere I go!"

"Really? Aren't you worried about your independence?"

"What's there to be worried about? I can still choose when I turn it on or off. But when I do connect, I'll have direct access to the vast amounts of information in Nexus! Not only that, but I'll be Linked with every other person who is currently synchronous! It's essentially a virtual reality! You can't tell me you don't think that is amazing. And it's *perfectly* safe!"

"I'm sure the operation will be perfectly safe," Appel conceded. "But what kind of assurances do they have so that your mind won't get lost in that virtual reality? Maybe you will like it better in this new experience. So much that you decide never to come out. Meanwhile, your body will be wasting away to nothing."

"I'm not that stupid," Lazarus said defensively. "Besides, they have fail-safes to prevent that."

"I don't mean it like that. I know you're not stupid. I just, I like to be the only one in my own mind. I like to know that my thoughts are my own and no one else's. Don't you want that?"

"Well sure, but I've been alone with my own thoughts all my life. I'm ready to let other people in now."

"Well, if that's what you want... how are you going to explain it to the rest of the crew? You know Raynor is a bit of a technophobe. He hates cyborgs and it's a wonder he doesn't have any issues with Abel. How do you think he will react to this?"

"He can just deal with it," Lazarus growled. "I'm not living my life to please him or anyone else."

"Oh, I see," Appel answered timidly.

Sensing her withdrawal from the conversation, Lazarus decided to try and change the subject. "Anyway, how have things been for you recently? It must have been hard for you since Reen was taken away."

"It has been," she confirmed. "No one has even really bothered to ask before now. It's like they are all scared to be seen talking to me with Lisa around."

"Well, at least they stood up for you when Swift wanted to haul you off for your involvement," Lazarus suggested. "What do you think they will do to him?"

Appel fell silent again. She wondered where he was going with all these questions about Reen. It certainly wasn't making her feel any better.

"I mean, I knew you both were doing some edgy research, but I never realised he wanted to try and turn us all into mutants," Lazarus continued.

"That's not what we were doing," she snapped. She shook her head. Lazarus obviously had no idea what the experiments were actually about. Why would he? She wondered whether the rest of the crew felt the same way.

Lazarus gave her a pitying look. "I'm sorry, I know he was your friend."

"What do you want me to say? He was my mentor. I helped him do what he wanted. None of it was my fault."

"I never said it was your fault," he insisted.

She looked at Lazarus seriously and wondered if she truly knew him well enough to explain this properly. "Reen was a really dedicated scientist. He was a nice person. Not that monster you saw being dragged out of the infirmary. He did what he did. He was dying. And, in the end, he sacrificed everything because he was trying to make humanity better. He wanted to unlock all the untapped potential we have inside of us. That's why I helped him."

"You know, you don't have to carry this burden alone," Lazarus said softly. "We're all in this together."

For a moment she wished he could read her mind and know the real burden she was dealing with. Then, as if he were reading her mind, he added. "Why don't you come with me? Come and get your Link upgraded too. We can do it together!"

"Do you have any secrets, Laz?"

He looked at her quizzically. "Not really. Why? What has that got to do with anything?"

"On the *Galaxy,* there are so many secrets. Every one of us has them. *Galaxy* was created to protect secrets from the Colonies."

"That's not *Galaxy's* purpose!"

"No? Well, I'm telling you, that's Rob, Raynor and Diputs' purpose. And they are the ones who created it. *Galaxy's* purpose is to move sensitive cargo for the Colonies, in secret! How do you think it will go down if you get a Synchronous Link? Suddenly you'll be a liability to what *Galaxy* is all about."

"What about Lisa? She *is* synchronous!"

"Lisa is already a liability. I understand your desire to be part of something bigger, to feel connected to some great digital consciousness. But you don't need an implant in your head to do that."

Appel reached out and gently placed her hand on top of his. Lazarus looked up at her and seemed surprised by her tender touch, but he didn't pull away. His eyes met hers and her heart started to pound wildly in her chest, a floodgate of emotions opened up for the first time since she could remember. Suddenly, his gentle expression turned to shock and surprise. He looked up behind her and before she could turn to see what he was looking at, they were both hit by the shock wave of an explosion that knocked them to the ground.

Lazarus leapt to his feet. "What was that?"

Before Appel could say anything, an alarm sounded that rumbled throughout the station with deep pulsating tones. A computer voice sounded out a status report. "Warning! Explosion detected in sector 12. Laser lift functions are non-operational. Nexus offline. Please remain calm and wait for further instruction."

It seemed as though everyone had ignored the notice. Appel could hear screaming and shouting all around her. Someone nearby yelled out that the station was under attack. Her mind flickered quickly. If they were under attack, what should they do? What *could* they do?

Lazarus grabbed her by the hand and pulled her up. They watched the previously quiet area suddenly flood with bodies as people spilt out of the structures around them. "Come on, we need to get back to *Galaxy*!" he shouted.

Appel couldn't even remember which way they had come or how to get back, so she allowed Lazarus to lead the way through the hordes of people. It seemed like they were all heading to the same place. She remembered that this station should have escape pods which could probably hold a few hundred people each, so surely the crowds would start to dissipate as people found their way off. Why did they all seem to be heading to the ship docks instead?

People were pushing and shoving all around her. All she had to do was keep following Lazarus, who had a firm grip on her hand. But even though he was only an arm's reach away he was still barely visible through the masses of panicking people. Appel stumbled and nearly lost her balance. If it weren't for everyone being so tightly packed together, she surely would have fallen over.

She looked down in horror to realise that she was standing on a body. She felt her stomach wrench and she wanted to throw up. She covered her mouth and held it in. That's when it hit her; she was no longer holding Lazarus' hand. She looked around frantically but could not make him out of all the hundreds of other faces surrounding her. She screamed his name, hoping he would at least hear it and turn back. But there was too much noise. There were too many people yelling and she could barely hear herself, let alone Lazarus. Tears stung her eyes as the realisation set in. She was lost.

DATAFILE

Anatomy of a Cyborg

NODE 1

Gen II Cyborgs are grown specifically for cybernetic enhancement, which is introduced into their bodies as they are grown in a controlled lab environment. This has the advantage of being able to completely replace many of their organs with mechanical systems while keeping a mostly human organic structure.

NODE 2

The brain: enhanced by improving the processing speed of thoughts and accessibility of data (such as memories). Enhancements include: Synchronous Neural Link, Enhanced Neural Synapses, Central Processing Unit, and Optic implants with an Augmented Reality interface.

NODE 3

Central Systems Core: most major organs have been replaced with a more efficient mechanical alternative. Core system enhancements include: Oxygen Generation and Nanite Circulatory System, Air turbines and oxygen compression tanks, Food/Organix energy converter, and reserve power cells.

NODE 4

Additional Enhancements: Hands - Vibrational sensors, and Interface touch connection. Genetic enhancements - Dense bone structure, and Enhanced Muscular System.

CHAPTER EIGHT

Inquisition

Lisa stood by the viewing portal in the Event Hall, observing the mob of delegates descending into panic and despair around her. She could feel something pushing at her mind, like a wave of vexation that stopped her from thinking clearly. Even though she was aware of it, she just couldn't seem to block it from her mind. She tried to focus, but her thoughts kept wandering back to Swift. It wasn't like him to miss an appointment. She knew he always detested these social events, where he had to try and 'behave' like a Supreme Commander. As if actually doing the job he was commissioned to do wasn't enough for people. She had tried to Link to him, but she couldn't seem to focus on getting a connection.

The people around her were some of the smartest minds in the colonies, yet when they had witnessed the escape pods floating through space, everyone had erupted into shouting accusations like a bunch of angry children. The crowd got violent. People pushed and shoved each other. Someone suddenly threw a punch and the room erupted into chaos. Lisa remained still, silently watching.

Swift's mech suit shimmered as he phased into full view of the congregation. He had been standing there the whole time, watching everything; undetectable by everyone through his chameleon plated armour. It deceived Even Lisa's enhanced optics.

Swift swooped down and lifted Clarissa back to her feet. Lisa felt a moment of jealousy. She didn't know whether to be angry or upset, so she decided to let both emotions envelop her. He had specifically told her to wait for him here. But instead of meeting with her, he had been there silently watching while she waited, feeling like a fool. She realised he had technically been there all along like he said he would. But this didn't detract from the sting of rejection she felt searing through her body. She turned away, annoyed by the revelation of Swift's actions. Determined to ignore the argument that Swift was cultivating with his presence.

She scanned over the ferocious crowd and spotted Raynor. He was following an older man dressed in a Lunar Colony uniform. Raynor grabbed the man's shoulder to halt him. Lisa read his lips, curious about the hostility in his action.

"Did you do this? Is this all about exposing Swift?" Raynor asked.

Lisa couldn't see the man's response. He had an intensity about him as he spun back around. He pushed his way towards the centre of the argument now taking place between Swift and Dalton. Raynor glanced around the Event Hall suspiciously, like he was up to something. His eyes didn't stop on her and he hurried off in the direction he had come from.

Lisa pushed through the crowd. Once she was clear, she stepped lightly, running cautiously up a ramp to the next level. This area was far less open than the one below. Only a single narrow passageway, lined with arches that separated closed doorways. She followed the passage until she found Raynor standing at one of the entrances. She hid behind an arch to avoid being seen and peered out cautiously to watch him place his Link on the panel next to the door. After a few quick taps, the interface lit up green. With a faint hiss, the door slid open. Lisa didn't want to enter right after him, so she waited. Her intent was to catch him in the middle of something incriminating.

She closed her eyes to connect with the doorway controls. For some reason, she still couldn't gain access to anything, not even Nexus. Whatever Raynor was doing it seemed he had planned this through exceptionally well. She would need to use an interface, so she placed her hand on the glowing surface. Nothing happened. A sudden violent urge captured her and she punched the panel with a closed fist, shattering its surface. There was no logical reason why her credentials wouldn't let her override the lock. Now she had no hope of getting in this way. Whatever Raynor was doing, it was most certainly illegal. She needed to gain access into the chamber.

There was an outline of an access panel on the ceiling. Lisa jumped up, boosted herself off the wall, and wedged her fingers into the gap. She was then able to force the panel open and pull herself inside the narrow service passage. She slid along the confined area until she reached a grate preventing her from going any further. She grabbed the bars and tried to break them. Her enhanced strength enabled her to bend the bars, but it was not enough. Additional nanites surged to her arms and hands as she struggled. Then the bars snapped out of place. The sudden and loud noise made her freeze. Listen. Raynor might have heard it. She pulled another one, this time with more care not to make as much noise. The bar bent, instead of snapping. The gap was now big enough for her to proceed. She pulled herself over to an air vent above the chamber. She looked down and saw that she was above Raynor. She moved the vent gently, just enough to get a better view of him working away on an interface.

He stopped what he was doing and looked up from the terminal. Lisa froze and slowed her breathing. He looked around and then went back to what he was doing. She watched as he brought up some information on the interface. She couldn't see it from her vantage point, but she could hear a voice from an audio file that he was playing.

"We can't really be thinking about using this, can we? This is madness."

Then another voice spoke. "We have no choice! All is lost, this is the only way."

The audio cut out as he grabbed a data crystal from the terminal and then left in a hurry.

Lisa opened the vent and dropped down into the chamber. She looked around at the artworks and relics lining the walls. Whoever resided here was obviously obsessed with the origins of humankind and the homeworld.

She got to work accessing the interface's recent activity. This terminal gave her unrestricted access to all the station's operations. Raynor had attempted to cover his tracks but Lisa knew all the tricks. He had accessed some encrypted files as well as some of the M1 system reports. There were hundreds of errors and faults coming from the control centre. She wondered about the voices she heard, so she checked the communications logs. Nothing was registered since before this all started. If Raynor was communicating with someone, it wasn't using conventional methods. She tried to fit all the pieces together, but she still felt foggy. She didn't have time to dwell on it, not if she wanted to keep up with him.

She exited the chamber just in time to catch sight of Raynor dashing down the long corridor. He no longer seemed to be in a hurry but every now and then he turned back to see if he was being followed. Luckily, her fast reflexes and the architecture of the arches scattered through the hallways allowed her to remain undetected.

After a while, Lisa began to wonder if Raynor even knew where he was going. He seemed to be wandering around in circles through the maze which was the inner workings of the observation decks. She had dropped quite far behind, so she picked up her pace to catch him. She realised she had lost sight of him and before she could slow herself, she experienced a sharp impact, then fell flat on her back.

Raynor looked down on Lisa sprawled out gracelessly on the ground. Despite his anger at being followed and spied on, he didn't feel good about ambushing and attacking her.

"Lisa!" He exclaimed, trying to sound surprised. "What were you doing? I thought you were one of them."

Lisa regained her feet quickly. Her eyes burned with hatred for him. "One of *them*?" she shook her head. "You can't just attack someone like that, what's come over you?"

"I didn't know who was following me," he lied. "What did you expect would happen? Something strange is going on here, I didn't want to take any chances."

Raynor offered her a hand up, but she slapped it away and got up on her own.

Lisa laughed ironically. "Don't you mean, you knew you'd been caught so you tried to take me out before I could expose you to Swift?"

"Look, I don't know what you think is going on here, but I'm not behind this."

"What exactly is *this*? You seem to know a lot for someone who's not behind it. What were you doing back there sneaking around in the curator's private room?"

Raynor crossed his arms. "We don't have time for this. I need to find Rob. He will know what to do."

Lisa looked at him sceptically. She seemed to be carefully considering his words. "He is probably already making his way to the control centre with Swift," she said. "I briefly overheard discussions as such while I was leaving to follow you. So, I'm sure Swift will handle whatever it is you are worried about. Anyway, how do you think you are going to help exactly?"

When he didn't answer right away, Lisa continued. "Who were you listening to back there? What were they talking about? What does it mean that all has been lost? Why is any of it relevant to what is happening here?" She grabbed him by the collar of his jacket and shook him. "What is going on with all of the internal systems? I am locked out of everything!"

Raynor could see the frustration contorting her face. She wasn't even giving him a chance to answer. He was glad she couldn't read his mind. "Don't worry about any of that, it's totally unrelated. I was with Bainsby when the escape pods ejected. He seemed to be acting strange, so I snuck back into his office to see what systems he had been accessing. The problem is he's covered his tracks pretty well."

"Better than you did, obviously. And what makes you think he was up to something? If he is the curator of *M1* why would he want to disrupt the Anamnesis? Maybe, just maybe, Bainsby is innocent, and you're insane!"

"Perhaps, but while I was there, I discovered that our orbit is decaying. Whoever has started this is trying to crash M1 into Lunar. He would have been able to see this and yet, he said nothing about it to me," Raynor admitted. "Even if he didn't cause it, he still knew about it from the start. He might have even caused the escape pods to launch!"

Lisa stood her ground. "Why would he do that?"

Raynor felt like her gaze pierce right through him. "Well, why would I be behind it? I don't want to die!"

"Let's just say I believe you. Then what? Why would Bainsby want everyone on here dead?" Lisa said. "None of what you are saying adds up."

"I know. It doesn't make any sense unless he has turned against the colonies and been brainwashed by outlaws. Why else would he destroy M1 while he was still on it? If what you say about Rob and Swift is true, then I guess there is nothing more we can do. We either wait for Rob to fix it or we are done for. Let's just sit here and find out, shall we? I mean it's not like you can report me to Swift right now. I'm sure he is a little busy."

Lisa's intense gaze started to wear him down.

"Look, you seem a little tense. I know we got off to a bad start, so why don't we go back to the Event Hall, get something to eat, sit down, relax, and wait for this whole thing to blow over? We can even try and work out our differences. I hear they have real food here, none of that Organix shit," he added, trying to ease the tension.

She looked insulted that he would even suggest such a thing at a time like this. He wondered if she had any sense of humour whatsoever.

"Hey, I was just joking. Why do you have to be so serious all the time?"

"Well, if there is nothing more we can do," she said, running her finger seductively down the side of his face. "And we're going to die regardless, right?"

Raynor raised one eyebrow, sceptical at her sudden change. She validated his scepticism with a right hook which connected to Raynor's jaw and knocked him backwards against the wall. He felt his lip and looked at the blood on his fingers. "So that's how it's going to be, is it? Don't even want to look at the menu?"

She hit him again, even harder this time. "Let's just say I've had a really shitty time, and I just don't like you. So, what's it going to be? Are you going to throw down with a cyborg in your last moments? Or are you scared?"

Lisa taunted him with a mischievous grin, which filled him with a burning desire. He couldn't believe that he was hearing this. All of a sudden, he didn't care about what happened to *M1*, or what consequences may occur if they survived. He wanted to fight Lisa more than anything else in this moment. He retaliated with a kick that hit her square in the stomach, pushing her backwards.

Raynor raised his fists and swung at her. She dodged it with ease and kicked the back of his knee, sending him to the ground. He scrambled back up and tried again, but she was still faster; countering with a direct blow to his face and following it up with a kick to the chest. Raynor went flying back. She ran at him ruthlessly and kneed him in the head. Raynor landed with a thud but took no time to recover.

Lisa circled him, a look of glee on her face. "Come on tough guy, is this all you got?"

He grabbed her ankle and tried to throw her off balance, but it was no use. Lisa dropped down on top of him and pummelled him with her fists over and over. She fastened one hand around his throat and squeezed.

"What is it you have been hiding from me?" She yelled between punches. "What have you and your shipmates really been up to?"

Raynor could feel his blood running down his face. He gritted his teeth. He wasn't going to tell her shit. He pivoted his hips, putting all the force he could muster into throwing her off. She fell beside him, and he tried to regain his footing.

Lisa had not felt this alive in a long time. She rolled over and then used the momentum to spring back to her feet. Raynor was a mess. She was surprised by his resilience. He just kept fighting back. Blood was flowing out of his nose and eyes. She went in for another attack and wondered how Swift would react to her killing his number one nemesis. Would he be happy? Or would he be annoyed that she had taken that opportunity away from him?

She put the thoughts to the back of her mind. She couldn't afford the distraction. Raynor had already landed a few decent kicks, which he capitalised on to gain the upper hand. He followed through by ramming her against the wall with his shoulder and punching her repeatedly in the head until she slouched down in defeat. He stood over her gasping for air. She wondered how Raynor still had so much strength left. After the beating she had dished out, he should be on the verge of death. But he just kept recovering. She could feel her strength waning. Those last few blows had taken a lot out of her and she suddenly wondered why she was doing this.

Raynor grabbed her by the shoulders and slammed her against the ground, pinning her arms down with his knees. She waited for another attack, but it never came. He just held her down, looking at her menacingly through his bloodshot eyes as he caught his breath.

For some reason, she no longer felt hatred towards him. Every muscle in her body ached and throbbed with pain. She had invited this.

Raynor eased the pressure on her arms, giving her some respite, but he didn't release her. A droplet of his blood rolled down his cheek and landed on her lip. He still gazed at her, unmoving. It no longer appeared to be a look of hatred or anger. What was it? Lust? Desire? Relief? Lisa didn't know what to do now. The fight was over, and she had lost.

She wondered what this would mean for her mission. No doubt if they survived this, Raynor would report her to their superiors and she would be in a fair bit of trouble. She couldn't imagine Swift would allow her to remain on *Galaxy* after this.

She reached up slowly and touched Raynor's lacerated cheek. "Stop," she whispered softly.

Raynor relaxed his grip and slumped down closer to her. Their faces were mere centrons from each other. He brushed back her hair, which was covering part of her face.

"There you are!" a chirpy voice exclaimed.

They both looked up to see Jake standing over them. Raynor quickly sat up, revealing the situation, to which Jake's bright cheer turned to a look of horror. He glanced back and forth between them trying to piece it all together.

"We're in big trouble, aren't we?" Jake queried.

"Don't worry about it," Raynor answered as he got up and walked away. "It's nothing."

Lisa, now alone, closed her eyes and listened to her cybernetic heart pumping. It worked above capacity to bring oxygen and fresh nanites to the rest of her body, which was now screaming at her as a result of the damage she had sustained. Raynor had done more damage than she had thought him capable of. She knew she should get up and go after him, but the threat of imminent danger drifted away as she fell out of consciousness.

GALAXY

CHAPTER NINE

Hostage

Diputs clenched his eyes shut. He heard and felt his heart pounding in his chest. His hands were still raised in front of his bloody face for protection. His cheek still stung from Scrubs wild fists.

"Get out of the way!" Scrub screamed, the anger piercing harshly through his words.

Diputs opened his eyes. He was still cowering on the floor of the laser lift bay. He was looking up at Serena, who had thrown herself in front of Scrub's aim.

"No! We can take him as a hostage," Serena pleaded.

"How will that help us?" Scrub said loudly.

Serena didn't seem to have an answer. "Why do you always want to kill everyone? That is not what the Divine wants. You know that!"

"But our mission is to kill everyone on board!"

"We are only meant to kill the colony representatives," Serena corrected him harshly. "We are not trying to kill innocent bystanders."

"Does it really matter? They are all going to die anyway."

"Of course it matters!"

"If we let him live, he is only going to hinder us."

"If we let him live, he might be of use to us," Serena said. "He is a ship's Operator. Surely he will be plenty of use back on Triton."

Scrub lowered his weapon slightly, but not his voice. "How do you even know he'll cooperate?"

"I know Diputs. He will do what is right," Serena said. She turned and looked directly into Diputs' eyes. "Won't you?"

Diputs weighed up his options; he could either agree with Serena or get shot. "Of course," He agreed. "I don't like the Colonies any more than you do."

Diputs felt confident in his answer. He resented the overbearing rules that the Colonies enforced. He also certainly planned to do what was right, but not for the outlaws, or the Colonies. Scrub didn't look convinced, so Diputs decided he should tread lightly.

Scrub still hadn't dropped his guard.

"Come on!" Serena pressed. "We don't have much time to get to the rendezvous point."

Scrub handed Serena a blaster and then pulled Diputs to his feet. Scrub then patted him down to search for any concealed weapons, putting no importance on his now useless Link.

Diputs watched the outlaw take a roll of binding tape from the equipment kit on the floor. He used the tape to restrain Diputs' hands behind his back.

"If he steps out of line, I want you to shoot him. Can you manage that Serena?" Scrub asked.

"Yes. Whatever it takes. But I don't think—"

"This way then," Scrub instructed and then led the way forward.

Diputs noticed Scrub was speaking quite loudly for someone trying to sneak around and guessed the explosion had damaged his hearing. He waited until Scrub was far enough ahead, then turned and whispered harshly to Serena. "Are you insane? I'm not going to join you. You are about to try and kill millions of people!"

"Look, I just needed a way to stop him from shooting you," she hissed. "Besides, that is a small price to pay for destroying all the evil that is on board."

"What *evil*?"

"You are all part of a slave society. You think you are free, but you're not," she said indignantly. "The Colonies only serve one purpose; to give you the illusion of freedom, while you give them your entire lives."

"What is the point in having freedom if you are just going to use it to kill a whole bunch of people?" Diputs asked. "You are only proving that you shouldn't have had it in the first place! You may not see it, but they got to you, and now you are in their mental trap."

"*Mental trap*? They helped my father after he got ill! He almost died!" Serena said, her face contorted in shock and disgust. "You knew he was sick and that I couldn't leave him to die. You still left to go on that stupid delivery ship, the *Universe*, or whatever, and expected me to go with you."

"It's called *Galaxy*," Diputs said louder, and knew it was a mistake.

Her eyes lit up with a glare of resentment that burned holes through his head. "How could you do that to me?" she spoke the words slowly and bitterly.

"Do that to you?" Diputs asked angrily. "I asked you to come with me, but you didn't have to. It wasn't an ultimatum. You could have stayed with your family and I would have still seen you when our schedules allowed it!"

"Hey! What are you chattering about?" Scrub called back. "You're holding us up. Is this going to be a problem? Because I can still splatter your brains all over the place if it is."

"No. It's just personal stuff. Things are just," Serena glanced at Diputs. "Complicated."

"I don't fucking care! We can't afford to get distracted!" Scrub looked directly at Diputs. "Let me make this real simple. Keep your voices down, keep walking, and don't get any brave ideas or else I'll end you. Got it?" Scrub waited for Diputs' nod of acceptance, turned back around and marched on.

Diputs waited some time before speaking to her again. A thousand arguments ran through his head. Then, once Scrub was further ahead, he asked in a hushed voice. "How did you ever get involved in this?"

She didn't reply right away. They walked silently through the empty service corridors. Then, after they emerged into a larger area with one wall looking out over the stars, she said, "The Divine has a purpose for us all, to create true freedom within Sol. We should all be working towards this. And these Revolutionists are the only ones who have any chance at all. I need to do this! The Divine healed my father. The Colonies would have let him die. They don't care about any of us!"

"None of what you said comes close to justifying taking these people's lives; innocent or not."

"Like I told you, it's a small sacrifice to free the people from their invisible prison."

"Are you listening to yourself? I thought you were smarter than this," Diputs whispered angrily. "They have totally brainwashed you! Don't you see?" Diputs held her hand. "This is not the way to freedom; you are only going to start a war. A war that will kill billions!"

"Whatever needs to be done, will be done," Serena insisted.

"What does that even mean? This is a war the outlaws can't win! Do you have a death wish or something? Let's say for a moment that this divine thing did heal your father. Do you want to have him and everyone else you love die in the war you start? Explain that logic."

"It is not my place to question the will of the Divine. He obviously has a bigger plan," Serena said. "I can't stand another minute living as a slave for the Colonies, which makes me an outlaw. Do you know what Enforcers do to outlaws?"

"It's no secret. They get taken to a correctional facility for re-education."

"No. You might believe those lies they feed you, but the truth is anyone who is not of value to the Colonies are executed. This is why the risk to me is worth it. If you joined us and felt the true power and love of the Divine, you would understand."

"That is utterly absurd," Diputs muttered.

"I'm willing to die for my beliefs. Are you willing to die for yours?"

They continued to walk in silence. The corridor widened. Red arrows appeared at the junctions; directions to the emergency exits. Dual pressure doors opened onto a broad concourse; the far wall lined with airlocks. Above each one, a status indicator flashed red.

Scrub stopped dead in his tracks. "No, they can't have."

Everyone stared at the empty escape pod terminals.

"They left without us," Serena murmured softly.

"No! They wouldn't do that," Scrub insisted as he searched the area. "They wouldn't, they—"

"All of the escape pods are gone!" Serena said, tears welling up in the corner of her eyes. "The plan was to launch them all at once so no one else could escape after us. They must have had to leave in a hurry. Maybe they were being chased?"

"No. They were supposed to wait for us. It doesn't make any sense!" Scrub said, falling to his knees. He dropped his blaster and buried his face in his hands.

"Not so fun now it's *your* lives on the line, is it?" Diputs mocked. "I guess this is part of the Divine will, too?"

"You shut your fucking mouth!" Scrub yelled. He picked up his weapon and launched himself at Diputs, grabbing him by the throat. He slammed Diputs against the wall with one hand, his blaster clenched in the other.

"Scrub! No!" Serena shrieked.

"I have a plan!" Diputs blurted.

"What did you say, motherfucker?" Scrub pressed the blaster harder into Diputs' skull.

"I said, I have a plan." Diputs felt Scrub relax his grip, allowing Diputs to breathe again. The sound of voices and footsteps echoed down the corridor from whence they came.

"That must be the Enforcers," Diputs suggested. "If you shoot me now, they will hear you and surge in, weapons blazing."

Scrub looked at the entry, then back at Diputs, uncertainty wavering in his eyes. Diputs wondered if this time he had pushed his luck too far.

Scrub took the blaster away from Diputs' head and pointed it at the doorway, but he did not release his grip on Diputs' throat. Diputs wriggled his hands, still in their bindings, to see if he could slip free. But it was no use.

The man who strode through the entrance was a tall man with sleek hair and a prominent moustache. He wore the uniform of an *M1* Steward, just like Serena and Scrub. So did the three men who followed him. One was even taller, the next was a bulky brute of a man, and the third was scrawny. None of them raised their weapons as they entered. They appeared to be assessing the situation by their puzzled looks.

"Civic! Thank the Divine! I knew you wouldn't have left without us. What happened to the escape pods?"

The defeated and helpless look on their faces was telling. Even though they said nothing, the awkward silence made it clear to Diputs that their plan had backfired somehow and left them all stranded.

"Who is this?" Civic asked, motioning towards Diputs.

"He is a friend of mine," Serena said. "He has a plan."

"A plan?" Civic asked, raising an eyebrow.

"Don't believe him," Scrub advised, waving his blaster back in Diputs' face. "He is up to no good. I can tell. He is just trying to trick us."

"Give him a chance," Serena pleaded. "I don't suppose you have a plan for how we can get out of this?"

Everyone looked at Scrub, waiting for him to voice a suggestion. Scrub opened his mouth, but no words came out. He looked down at his feet and said nothing.

Civic turned back to Diputs. "Let's hear it, then."

"I have a ship, *Galaxy*. It's in the docks on the other end of the station. Since you blew up the laser lifts, there is no easy way to get to it. But one of these equipment lockers around here should contain a space suit. I could make my way to the docks on the outside of the station and then come back and pick you up."

Civic twirled the edge of his moustache between his thumb and forefinger. "That sounds like a fine plan, except for one small detail. You see, if we let you go from here, I don't think we would ever see you again. Why should you come back for some freedom fighters? How about we find a few extra suits and just come with you? How does that sound?"

CHAPTER TEN

Stranded

Lazarus struggled to push his way through the crowds flowing over the Transway surface. There were a vast number of people all scampering to get to safety. It made him feel like he was being tossed down a violent river, struggling not to be pushed under and drowned.

He held on to Appel's hand as tight as he could, but the frenzied mob surged around them. Their hands began to rip apart, their fingers tangled with each other to try and stay connected. He gripped her as tight as he could, but still she slipped away. He could hear her calling out to him. He desperately tried to push against the flow of people that raged around him, it was near impossible. His shouts to Appel were already muffled, and he realised he had lost her.

The frantic horde knocked Lazarus to the ground and trampled over him. A foot landed heavily on his stomach, winding him. He could barely cry out in pain and the relentless stampede followed. He realised that he wasn't the only one to fall; there were other screams all around from other people who were getting crushed under the weight of the crowd. He reflexively raised his hands and curled up in a defensive ball. He knew if he didn't get out soon, he would die.

He searched around in a panic for something, anything to help him escape. Then he realised what he was lying on. He could see the stationary Transway cars through the transparent floor panel. He knew each panel would have a release for maintenance purposes, so he reached for an access latch and cursed when someone stepped on his wrist, mashing it into the ground. Another person stomped on his ribs. He gritted his teeth harder and pushed himself forwards to reach the latch. He managed to grip it and then wrenched with as much force he could muster. Nothing happened. He kept pulling and felt the panel shift down slightly. He pulled it again and slammed his fist down in frustration. The panel gave way and he fell along with several other people, their bodies crashing on top of a carriage just a few metrons under the Transway surface.

The long cylindrical carriages were lined with glass and contained seating and standing space for at least one hundred passengers. He looked around to assess the situation. Bodies lay strewn over the top of the carriage, some dead and others disoriented from the fall. Another person was hanging from the ledge and dropped to land clumsily on top of the carriage.

Every part of him hurt, but he forced himself to push his torso up with one arm allowing him to look for a way down. Others were now jumping down from above to get away from the crowd, so he dragged himself over to the edge and attempted to lower himself over the side of the carriage. He failed miserably and fell to the bottom of the Transway passage.

He felt something break. Maybe his ribs. He reached down to assess the damage and pulled out his Link. It was completely shattered. He didn't have time to worry about that now. He had to find a way to reach the docks.

Lazarus slowly found his feet and made his way over to a nearby terminal. He pried open the wall panel and started tampering with the circuitry. It was at least thirty floors below the surface level, and it occurred to him that if the Transway was down, then no one would be able to reach the loading floor of the ship docks. He accessed the primary node and hacked into the Transway grid. Then, he activated the manual override for the Nexus controlled navigation system. The lights on the carriage adjacent to them flickered on. He had to get going before everyone realised the Transway was back online and started to flood the carriages.

Lazarus steadied himself against the wall and then pushed off, ignoring the pain in his back and shoulders. He surprised himself by managing a brief run, in just a few moments he had reached the carriage. He looked back up at the Transway surface. There were so many trampled bodies. He couldn't see any that looked like Appel, but it was hard to tell. If Appel were still up there somewhere, it would be almost impossible to get to her.

Lazarus climbed into the carriage. "Ship docks, no stopping," he instructed the onboard interface. The carriage picked up speed and Lazarus looked out through the glass as other people in the Transway scrambled out of the path. Lazarus couldn't help feeling guilty for abandoning all the people to whatever fate awaited this station.

The carriage finally began the vertical descent to the boarding levels of the ship docks. He desperately wanted to go back and search for Appel, even though he knew he had no chance of finding her in all this chaos. He also spared a thought for the rest of his shipmates who had gone up for the Anamnesis. Would he ever see any of them again? What could he possibly do to help them if this really was some sort of attack?

"Level 34, ship docks, mezzanine," the automated voice said. Lazarus became aware of his surroundings once again and considered just how dazed he really was. He found his feet and stepped cautiously onto the platform. Pain surged through him once again, reminding him of his injuries.

The walk back to Galaxy seemed much further than when he had first arrived. About half of the ships that were first docked on M1 had already gone. He turned back when he heard shouts and screams. Other carriages were arriving, and people spilt out of them like a crashing wave, many of them setting their sights on the larger or closer ships in the docks. Carriage after carriage brought hundreds of extra people who flocked out into the gigantic landing. A movement caught his eye, and he looked across at where the *Galaxy* should have been, just in time to see it fly away.

DATAFILE

Medical Report, Dr Kinsley Diren - C1096 S22 R20

Patient: Resden Koran

Gender: Male

DOB: C1036 S08 R11

ID: M44892P7340093

Admitted Time: 22:06

Symptoms: Nausea, vomiting, dizziness, delirium, Sweaty and Clammy skin and Fainting spells

Diagnosis: Radiation Poisoning

Advised Treatment: Isolation from external environmental sources and detox through Olkamium alkaloids and medical discs D398, R82 and L37 to relieve pain.

Notes:

At 22:06 Resden Koran was admitted to Narku medical treatment facility on Lunar for a variety of unexplained symptoms. Blood test results came back with traces of Theridium Alpha, which is a rare form of radioactive material only found in the Kuiper Belt. As the patient has never been to the restricted area, it was ruled out as an impossibility and treated as a misdiagnosis. Further observations have been advised.

CHAPTER ELEVEN

Evacuation

Clarissa looked around the dimly lit service passages. The walls and floor were grey and bare. Red lights flashed on and off, warning of danger. She followed closely behind Swift, Rob and Persephone. Swift had led them up several floors, heading towards the control centre at the very top of the observation decks. It was eerily quiet in this part of the station, with no sign of any staff or guests. They stopped at a junction, which forked off in two different directions.

"Do you actually know where you are going, Swift?" Clarissa asked.

"Of course I do, don't be daft."

Swift looked around as if it would somehow help him get his bearings in the seemingly endless corridors. Each one looked exactly the same as the last, with no distinguishing features. They turned left, walked up another ramp and turned a corner to reveal large metal doors, framed by a strip of red light.

"Here it is," Swift announced. He pressed the interface panel beside the entrance to elicit a response from someone inside but there was no reply. After a few moments he tried again. Still no response.

"It's locked, Swift! Clearly, no one is in there. Do any of you have access permissions?" Clarissa asked.

"Well, no, but I can attach my Link to the interface then bypass the verification subroutines," Rob suggested.

"We don't have time for that," Swift insisted. Using the immense power of his mech suit he kicked violently at the door, leaving a large dent.

"No, really, it will only take a few moments," Rob insisted.

"We may not have a few moments," Swift added, kicking the solid metal doors again. He had created a small gap, enough to get his armoured fingers through. He peeled the doors open like they were made of wax. Then he stepped through the opening and looked around. "It's safe, come on in."

Persephone was the next to enter, followed by Rob.

"What happened here?" Persephone asked, scrunching up her face.

As soon as Clarissa entered, the stench of seared flesh overwhelmed her. She saw a body slumped over on the ground and ran towards it. She dropped to her knees and covered her mouth in shock. Severe burns covered his skin. She had to fight back her gag reflex at the gruesome sight of his empty eye sockets and crimson face. She scrambled back and was startled by another corpse. This one appeared to have met a different fate. Dark bruises around his crushed throat indicated that he had been choked to death. She tried to maintain control of her emotions, but her hands were shaking with grief.

"This is awful," Clarissa cried. "How could anyone do such a brutal thing?"

Persephone placed her hand gently on Clarissa's back which both surprised and comforted her.

"People can do unspeakable things," Persephone said. "I know it is upsetting but let's try to stay objective here, shall we?"

"How are you all so calm about this?" Clarissa asked. "Are you all really this desensitised to death?"

None of them answered, they only gave each other knowing looks. This certainly wasn't a first for any of them.

"All of the interfaces have been obliterated," Rob stated. "It's going to be difficult to get access to any of the systems."

"Can't you just connect to one using your Link?" Persephone asked.

"I'll try," Rob replied. "But there may be too much damage." He reached into one of the smashed interfaces and tugged on some circuitry. He produced a small, sharp tool from his coat pocket and proceeded to pry the back off his Link. He connected it to the interface using micro strands extruding from the shattered panel and tapped away at his Link. "Okay, I'm in," he said, beaming with satisfaction. It didn't last long. His expression changed to a look of panic as he read the data displayed to him.

Clarissa leant in close with everyone else to try and see what was happening, even though she didn't have the slightest idea of what any of it meant.

"What is it? What have you found?" Swift demanded.

Rob nervously cleared his throat and loosened his collar. "It looks like someone has fired the thrusters, pushing the station out of its orbit. On our current trajectory, we're going to crash into Lunar."

Clarissa gasped.

"You can fix it, right?" Persephone asked.

"Fire them the other way, you fool!" Swift ordered.

Rob's fingers worked quickly as he tried to gain access to modify the space station's course. "This thing is so old the orbital thrusters aren't responding. It's going to take me a bit of time to get them back online."

"What can we do?" Clarissa asked.

"Shut up and let me work!" Rob snapped.

"You know you really are some piece of work, Rob," Swift said.

Rob ignored the comment and kept working. So Swift went back to casually inspecting the damage around him. He took a few steps across the room and then stopped.

"Dammit," he said, covering his nose.

"What is it now, Swift?" Persephone asked.

Swift looked at his fingers. They were covered in blood. He took a few steps back. "That's strange," he said.

"What is? Are you okay?" Clarissa asked.

Swift walked closer to the far side of the control centre. He grabbed the sides of his head with both hands. "It's that box with the purple glow. The closer I get to it the worse my headache feels."

Persephone walked over to stand next to him. "I don't feel any different. My head feels fine. Maybe you should just toughen up."

"No, he's right," Clarissa said. "I thought it was just me. I started getting a headache just before the escape pods launched. I just figured it was from all the noise in the Event Hall. But as we made our way up here it just kept getting worse."

Persephone knelt and reached for the switches on the device's interface.

"Don't touch that, you fool!" Swift shouted. "Everyone in here is dead and you want to go poking a strange purple glowing box? Everyone take cover, I'll deal with this!"

He activated the visor on his mech suit and reached down to pull the power-node cable out from the side of the device. Arcs of electricity danced up his armour as he yanked the cable free. Clarissa felt instant relief as the pressure that had built up inside her head dissipated.

"My Link! I've got a connection!" Persephone yelled.

"My headache is gone!" Clarissa added.

Swift punched the machine with the full force of his mech suit, over and over again until the device was thoroughly destroyed.

"What did you do that for?" Persephone asked. "It was already disabled."

"This thing is dangerous. I'm making sure no one else can use it. It's called being prudent."

"Yeah, as long as it involves destroying something," Persephone added.

"I'm calling June," Clarissa said. "She was on her way back to Lunar, so hopefully she can provide some assistance." She watched the two rings spinning around an orb on her Link waiting for it to connect.

Finally, June's face appeared. "Clarissa! Where are you? Are you still on M1?"

"Yes, I'm in the control centre. Look, we have an emergency situation. We're—"

"I know," June said calmly. "We've been trying to make contact since we noticed *M1* changing course."

"So, what are you doing about it? How many ships are nearby? We need to evacuate as many people as possible!" Only silence followed. Clarissa realised the meaning behind June's reluctance to answer and choked on the words as she tried to say what June wouldn't. "You're not going to do anything, are you? You're... you're going to let us die."

"Clarissa, I'm so sorry," June said, breaking the silence. "There is nothing we can do. *M1* wasn't designed for re-entry into the atmosphere. On your current course your hull will collapse under the pressure of our gravity and you will burn up during descent."

For some reason she found herself looking to Rob for confirmation, as if there were some minute chance June could be wrong. She could see him programming a graph on his Link. It showed *M1* in relation to Lunar, with a dotted line connecting them. The masses of numbers that he typed into the screen were beyond her comprehension.

He looked up bleakly. "She's correct. Even with the thrusters at maximum, it's still not going to be enough to free us from the pull of the Lunar gravity."

"I am so sorry," June apologised again.

"That doesn't mean I can't fix it though," Rob added.

"What?" June and Clarissa gasped in unison.

"All of our simulations say it's impossible," June protested. "You really can't."

"You're just going to give up?" Clarissa asked.

"If you somehow manage to fix the entry angle, *M1* will still most likely break apart," June insisted. "Even if it doesn't burn up in the atmosphere, large chunks of the space station will come crashing down on Lunar and cause unimaginable destruction. Millions of people would die!"

"Yes, I can fix that too," Rob said, dismissing her argument with a flick of his hand.

"You can't do it!" June Insisted. "Trust me. I have had our best scientific minds assessing every possible outcome and *M1* landing safely in one piece isn't one of them!"

"Firstly, all of your best scientific minds are up here. Secondly, I'm smarter than any of them!" Rob stated.

June scowled. "If you change course, we will be forced to blow you out of the sky."

"Oh really?" Clarissa asked. "So how did you go getting your turret grid back online?"

She looked at Rob with a satisfied smirk.

June folded her arms. "It was our first priority. The ground defences are at full strength."

Clarissa could see by her body language that she was avoiding the truth. She started to feel a sliver of hope. "I don't believe you."

"Clarissa, think about this!" June pleaded. "Think about how many lives could be lost if he gets it wrong. The risk just isn't worth it to save one space station. You know that. You're a Peacekeeper."

Clarissa looked at Rob. "Can you look me in the eye and tell me this will work?"

"Yes. I have a plan to stabilise the hull. It's going to be a nail-biting ride, but I am certain I can pull this off. I'll send you our estimated landing path. If I were you, I'd start evacuating all of your towers near the coastline."

"Thanks for your help then, June," Clarissa said, then ended the link and looked at each of them. "We can do this!" she said, hoping that her belief would make it true.

"Dammit," Rob said.

"What? What is it?" Clarissa asked.

"My ship is still in the docks." Rob opened a link to *Galaxy*. "Red, what are you still doing on *M1*? It's going to crash!"

"Waiting for everyone to return," Red replied dutifully.

"Never mind that, just depart. Now!"

"My scanners have picked up life signs located outside the space station. Diputs is out there, should I recover him?"

"What's he talking about?" Swift asked. "Why, and how, is Diputs on the outside of the space station?"

He activated the visor on his mech suit, which encased his head with armoured glass. Clarissa could see a holographic display projected on the front of it.

"There are others as well!" Swift said. "The Link signatures are of Lunar origin by the looks of it. I knew this was some sort of inside job."

"How can you possibly know that? Everyone is trying to escape the station, but that doesn't make them guilty of sabotage," Rob argued.

"I bet Diputs is taking his buddies to *Galaxy* to escape," Swift said. "Too bad for you, it looks like he is planning to leave you behind to die along with the rest of us. Well, I'm not letting him get away with it."

"If you go out there now the gravity will pull you down to the surface with *M1* and you will burn up," Rob warned.

"Unlike their standard issue space suits, my mech suit can withstand reentry. I'll be fine," Swift called out as he left the control centre in hot pursuit of his prey.

"Red, did you get all of that?" Rob asked.

"I'm on my way now. However, Diputs is a fair distance away. Swift has a good chance of reaching him first."

"Just go!" Rob ordered, cutting the connection.

"Diputs!" Persephone shouted into her Link. "Thank goodness you're alright, what are you doing out there?"

The slightly distorted voice replied, "I've been taken hostage by outlaws and—"

"Swift is en route. Just try and hang back—"

"No! This isn't what it looks like... you need to hold him off."

Rob snatched the Link out of her hand. "Red is already on his way to get you. Just hold tight and try not to get shot." Then the connection dropped.

Persephone stowed her Link and ran for the exit.

"Where are you going?" Clarissa asked.

"I have to go after Swift!" Persephone said, slipping into a space suit pulled from a wall-locker. "Diputs is going to need my help. You heard him; he's just an innocent bystander swept up in all of this."

"I need to contact Laz and Appel," Rob said. "I don't want them to think we've left them to die."

Only one face appeared on his Link. Appel looked to be surrounded by an immense crowd. Her face looked flushed and fear filled her eyes. "Rob! Where are you?" she asked.

"Never mind that, where are you? Are you with Laz? I couldn't Link to him."

"No, I lost him," she said. Her voice breaking on the words. She looked away. "I'm in the ship docks. I just saw *Galaxy* fly off."

"Yes, I'm sorry," Rob said. "The space station is going to crash into Lunar. I had to get *Galaxy* to safety. Had I known you were so close, I—"

"You did what you had to. It's fine."

"I am still here too, pretty much the entire crew is. I have a plan to save everyone. Trust me," Rob assured her.

"So what is it?"

"There isn't time to explain. Get out of the docks and find somewhere close to a suspension field emitter."

The conversation didn't exactly fill Clarissa with confidence. She was beginning to wish she had followed Swift and Persephone, who would no doubt be rescued by one of the ships nearby. But if she were to leave now, she would be abandoning everyone on board, including her father. Rob may yet need her help. He could have left too, but he stayed to do everything in his power to try and save as many people as possible.

She envied Rob and the relationship he had with his crew. They obviously cared so much for each other that they would risk their lives in such a way. Who cared for her, apart from her father? June was clearly not all that concerned. Eryn was supposedly so in love with her yet said nothing when she volunteered to accompany

Swift to the control centre. He hadn't even bothered to Link to her to see if she was alright. She decided that if she survived this, she would not let him forget how he had neglected her during this crisis.

CHAPTER TWELVE

Conduit

Raynor stood next to Jake in the Event Hall with the guests of the Anamnesis. He noticed some sneak away, probably for some last-minute goodbyes. He felt somewhat helpless, but knowing Rob and Swift were in the control centre working to try and solve their dilemma was somewhat comforting. He had already gone to the laser lift bays and looked out at the city far below. There was nothing else he could do. So there he was, swirling a glass of synthetic wine in one hand and a skewer of spiced meat in the other. He waited to find out if this rotation was the one he was going to die. He wondered what Lisa was doing since he had left her on the floor bruised, bloodied and broken. He tried not to feel bad about it. After all, she was the one who had attacked him.

Some of the guests were still arguing feebly over whose fault it was. Not that it mattered now. They were all as good as dead anyway. He was startled when his Link buzzed from his utility belt. He grabbed it with an entirely explicable urgency. "Rob! Please tell me you have some good news!"

"Look, I don't really have time to explain everything, but I need your help to crash *M1* into Lunar."

Raynor sure hoped his friend was joking. Rob always had the worst sense of humour in these situations. "Have you lost your mind? It was already crashing. You were meant to be stopping it!"

"It's not that easy. If we don't stabilise the hull, the station will break apart and probably explode. Have you still got that thing with the weird energy readings? That one you discovered recently?"

"Of course I do. Why, what do you want with it?"

"Never mind, there is a power substation near the observation decks. I need you to go there and divert power from all other systems into the suspension fields, gravity networks and the thrusters. I'm going to try and crash land into the Lucidian Ocean. Link me when you get to the substation!"

Raynor knew better than to question Rob's logic. He immediately set off with a new enthusiasm to not die. He looked back to make sure Jake was following and was surprised that the lad was right behind him.

Once they had cleared the frightened crowd, Raynor and Jake sprinted down a curved corridor and up an incline to the next level. Raynor hesitated briefly while he recalled the map in his head and then set off again, leading them up yet another floor to the substation. He hacked his way past the locked door with ease and they entered onto a platform overlooking six giant cylindrical power assemblies, connected by a metal walkway. Each assembly contained a power coupling which surged with energy drawn from the main reactor to power the observation decks. There was an interface on the railing across from them, which Raynor approached without delay.

"Okay, I'm here. What do I need to do now?" Raynor asked into his Link.

"Open the power settings and turn everything off except for the gravity systems. Then I want you to go in and turn off all the safety settings and overload limits," Rob instructed carefully.

"Yes, then what?"

"Then I want you to go over to one of the power couplings and switch it to input from an external source."

Raynor made his way over to the closest power coupling, removed the clear protective panelling and gazed into the raw surging power inside the structure. He flipped the switch but nothing happened. He toggled the switch back and forth a couple of times, but still nothing. "Rob. It's not doing anything."

"Shit! You need a way to bridge the connection. I was sure it would've just picked up on the energy from that item you are carrying."

Raynor took the Artifact out of his pocket and pressed it against the input panel. Still nothing happened. "What do you mean by *bridge* the connection?"

"You know, try to find some way to connect it to the power assemblies. You may need to throw the item into the energy stream."

"I'm not letting the Artifact go, Rob! This thing is far too valuable."

"We don't have a choice, Raynor. If you don't do it we are going to die!"

"What if I bridge the connection?" Raynor asked hopefully.

"Then you'll die! Don't do it, Raynor, the Artifact isn't worth dying for!"

Raynor shut off his Link. He had heard enough. He grasped the artifact in his left hand and squeezed it tight. He placed his fist slowly into the chamber of the assembly above the power coupling. He tried to let it go, but his fist refused to open. He looked over to Jake, still on the platform watching intently. Raynor withdrew his fist and plunged his other hand down onto the exposed coupling. He let out an almighty scream as the power surged through him.

DATAFILE

Link connected; 18:10 C1099 S5 R2

Transcription:

"Father, how is everything going down there?"

"Clarissa, my dear. You've got the communications up! Please tell me everything's under control up there now. It was getting pretty hairy in here at one point, but I managed to settle everyone down. It's like they all just ran out of anger."

"You might want to step out, so no one else can listen to what I am about to say."

-Brief pause-

"Okay, go ahead."

"Someone has killed all of the Operators up here. They have pushed *M1* out of orbit and we are about to plunge into the Lunar atmosphere."

"There must be something we can do. We need to contact Lunar, right away!"

"I have, father. They aren't in a position to help us. Rob, the scientist who came with us, has a plan to try and land us safely but it's risky."

"Risky? Clarissa, I'm sorry but I just don't think—"

"I just wanted to tell you how sorry I am about our argument earlier. I know you were just trying to do the best thing for everyone, including me. I love you dad, and when we survive this, I will try to become as good of a Peacekeeper as you."

"Clarissa, I love you too, I am so proud of you!"

-End of communication-

CHAPTER THIRTEEN

Escape

A bead of sweat ran down Diputs' forehead. Being stuck in a space suit meant he was unable to wipe it away. Walking down the hull of the massive space station with magnetic boots was tiring work. For each step, he had to lift his foot in just the right way to disengage one of the magnetic locks keeping him from floating into space.

A connection request popped up in his HUD with a red border. It was from Persephone. "Diputs! Thank goodness you're alright, what are you doing out there?"

A wave of relief washed over him. "I've been taken hostage by outlaws and—"

"Swift is en route. Just try and hang back—"

"No! This isn't what it looks like... you need to hold him off."

Persephone looked confused, but didn't have a chance to react before the screen jittered and Rob appeared in her place. "Red is already on his way to get you. Just hold tight and try not to get shot." Then the connection dropped.

Diputs could feel his heart throbbing in his chest and anxiety building in his stomach.

"Link; proximity find, Serena Koran." The display in his visor told him that no one by that name was in close proximity. He remembered she wasn't using her real name. Her Link was probably encoded with fake identification. "Link, proximity find, display all." His visor displayed the link Id's of all the outlaws around him. He read through them all; Brute, that must have been the big guy. Civic was the leader. He tried to also put faces to Lannek and Pulse. Scrub he already knew. Then he saw *Glitch* and remembered hearing it when he first bumped into Serena. "Hey," he said after she accepted the connection. "We're in trouble. We need to surrender, right now."

Serena stopped in her tracks. She turned slightly so she could look directly at him. "Surrender to who? And why? We're almost there."

Diputs watched the other outlaws stop and turn to look at him and Serena. He opened his communication to everyone, then raised his arms and placed them over his head. "We have been discovered, you need to surrender, or you'll be killed. Please, just do it!"

Lannek raised his blaster, taking aim. "There is no surrender, only death!"

His helmet exploded as a high-velocity round passed right through it, splattering his brain all over the visor. A trail of blood followed the bolt out into space. It was one of the most horrific things Diputs had ever seen. The suit's display tracked the trajectory of the shot and Diputs turned his whole body to follow it back to the source. The friend or foe system automatically painted Swift as an ally, charging towards their position.

The outlaws reacted by sending a barrage of fire back in Swift's direction.

"Die you fucking colonist bastard!" Civic yelled through his Link.

Diputs and Serena ducked behind a thruster protruding from the hull plating to avoid the projectiles that whizzed past. He was startled when the thruster exploded with bright blue energy causing everything to shake violently. Rob must have regained some control in a futile effort to prevent, or at least prolong, the inevitable crash. But Diputs estimated that it was already too late. The entire structure trembled under the stress of the Lunar gravity. He could only hope that *Galaxy* was not far away. He watched another outlaw get picked off by Swift with a shot to the chest. Diputs could hear his screams through the still-open connection as the outlaw's lungs filled with blood.

"Get up, you faithless scourge. This is all your fault!"

Diputs received a push in the back of his helmet. He turned slightly to try and see who, but was prodded once again, harder this time.

Serena screamed, "no, Scrub! Don't do it!"

Out of the corner of his eye Diputs could see her take aim at him.

"Serena, don't!" Diputs pleaded. "Put it down, it's not worth it!"

She fired three shots at him. Diputs assumed at least one of them made its mark when the push on the back of his helmet went away. Time seemed to slow down. His eyes glanced back over towards Swift. There was another soldier flying towards them. Another ally, shooting at him. Diputs's suit tracked the hyper-accelerated smart round as it tore through Serena's helmet and trailed off into space beyond. As her suit ruptured, she desperately tried to breathe, but the vacuum of space sucked the air out of her lungs. Her veins darkened around her face and her arms went slack. She looked at Diputs one last time, and then she was gone.

Diputs' heart sank. He looked into her lifeless eyes. No last words, no goodbyes, no closure, just death. The damage to her suit uncoupled the magnetic lock on her boots and her body drifted away slowly.

"Diputs!" Persephone yelled. Her voice thundered through his helmet, interrupting his moment of despair. "Diputs, are you okay? It's over now."

Diputs didn't reply. He felt sick. He remembered Serena telling him that she was willing to die for what she believed in. He wondered if this was what she meant. Had she sacrificed herself because she believed in him?

Persephone grabbed him by the shoulders and released the magnetic lock on his boots. Diputs saw her look at him with what seemed to be genuine concern. She pushed off from the station and pulled him into space with her.

In a flash, it all came to him. All of the pieces fitted together. She was the soldier flying with Swift. She was the one who had shot Serena. He felt outraged. He wanted to scream at Persephone. Why did she have to kill Serena? But instead of anger, he buried himself deep in his sorrow. Persephone couldn't possibly have known who Serena was. It would have simply appeared as a hostage situation, with two outlaws pointing guns at him.

Diputs looked up as they drifted closer towards a large ship. The entry doors were open, and he could see the blue suspension field that sealed the air and pressure inside. It wasn't *Galaxy*; this ship was much larger. Large enough to be a warship.

CHAPTER FOURTEEN

Turncoat

Swift retracted his helmet once they had passed through the suspension field. A wave of relief swept over him. He was glad to be finally back on Goliath. Now he could take control of the situation. Several of his men were standing at attention. They were led by Romuel, his second in command, no doubt here to see that his fearless leader had returned unharmed.

Swift moved deeper into the lobby. Robotic arms sprung out of the floor to disassemble his armour, freeing him from its confines. He had noticed Persephone watching as he changed into a fresh uniform, so he gave her a sly smile. Persephone, Diputs and the outlaw were still in their space suits. Diputs stared blankly at the floor in silence. Swift thought he seemed awfully glum for someone who was spared from death. The outlaw was just as quiet, no doubt mourning for his friends. That is, he pondered, if those wretched outlaws even had feelings.

"Take these two criminals to a holding cell, the woman is free to go," he instructed his subordinates.

"Go where?" Persephone complained. "Diputs is a victim in all of this. They were holding him as a hostage. You can't just lock him up!"

"Oh, how convenient, just a hostage," Swift mocked. "I guess we'll let him go then, shall we? There's no need to question him? Maybe try to verify his story? How stupid are you?" He turned to Romuel. "Take them away."

"And me?" Persephone gasped.

"You will be dropped off at our next port of call, at a time convenient to our schedule. Until then, I don't know, just stand there and be quiet."

Persephone gave him a look that he thought was quite unflattering. He was tired of this conversation, so he made his way towards the control centre.

Swift's Link buzzed while he was on route. He held it in front of his face and tapped to answer it.

"Swift, we need your help!" the woman began.

"What do you want, June?"

"I'm glad to see you are safely back on Goliath. Now I need you to blow up M1."

"Destroy it? Why?"

"You know why. Think about how much damage that thing will do when it hits the surface."

"So, why don't you destroy it? Oh, that's right, something about your defence grid being disabled. Shame about that. I do hope some of your warships can make it in time. Surely they have enough fire power."

"How could you know that? Ah, you were in the control centre on *M1* when I spoke to Clarissa!"

"What does that matter?"

"Well, I'm just wondering how much the Supreme Commander of the Martian Fleet had to do with the sabotage and ultimate destruction of the *M1 Space Station*. Not to mention the numerous Lunar cities that will be destroyed as a result. This could be considered an act of war you know!"

Swift realised he had let his gloating get the better of him. Now it seemed that June had the upper hand. She had him by the balls now.

Or did she?

"June please, everyone of any importance is on that space station. If I destroy it there won't be anyone left for me to answer to. Besides, there's a chance that Rob will actually succeed!"

"There is a greater chance that he won't! Come on Swift, quit stalling and just do it! I know you have people you care about on *M1*, I do too, but the billions of lives on Lunar are more important!"

The last comment jarred him. People he cared about on *M1*? Did she mean Lisa? How could she possibly know about Lisa? Regardless, it wasn't long ago that he had opened fire on a stolen Martian warship, all the while knowing that his love was on board. He had done that with no hesitation whatsoever. But that was different, this time he was safe no matter what the outcome. He also thought about all of the Martian representatives and Peacekeepers. What would happen to the colonies if they all died at his hands? How would the other colonies ever trust the Martians after that? It would result in destruction of the Nexus. Peace between the colonies would be broken once again, threatening his home and his people. But his role was simple; protect Mars. He wasn't responsible for the other colonies. On the other hand, if

Rob failed and everyone on *M1* died as well as the destruction of a Lunar city, there would still be war. It seemed as though he would probably be blamed either way.

"Swift, we are running out of time!"

"Shut up, I'm thinking about it." He ended the Link and strode into the control centre on Goliath. "Prepare the Disseminator."

He thought about Linking to Lisa. No, that would be too sappy. Instead, he felt strangely compelled to contact Clarissa. She was so full of hope that they could survive this. It seemed only right to give them fair warning. Then she could break the news to everyone else. He sat down in his command chair. "Link me to Clarissa Dalton, bring it up on the main viewing portal."

"Swift, what is it?" Clarissa asked. "We have already begun our descent."

"I know and I'm sorry. I have to end this," he said, trying to sound genuinely forlorn.

"Swift, don't you dare! Rob's plan is working! The station is holding. We can make it!"

He hesitated. Could this be true? He pushed softly on a tiny interface embedded in his chair and scanned the hull integrity. Rob had somehow activated every single suspension field generator on *M1* and had used them to create a gravity field around the entire station. What he was seeing seemed impossible, but then again, he wasn't exactly a scientist.

"I'll make it worth your while," Clarissa pleaded to the silence.

"What do you mean?"

"If you let us do this, I will make sure none of your fleet is taken as tribute."

"You can't do that, can you?"

"Yes, I can, I'm a Peacekeeper! Besides, if I survive this, I will be forming a unity with Eryn Jaines. The soon to be UAE Fleet Commander. So, he will be answering to me from now on."

Swift looked around at the rest of his crew, waiting for any reason why he shouldn't listen to her.

"You have it recorded sir. If by chance they don't make it, you have a verbal agreement with a Peacekeeper. Even if she is still only in guidance," Romuel advised.

"Well then, in that case, you have a deal. Happy crashing."

Clarissa's face vanished from the viewing portal and their deal was done.

"Power down the Disseminator and get us out of here. Now!"

CHAPTER FIFTEEN

Devastation

Lisa snapped back into awareness. She looked around the corridor, remembering that she had just been in a fight with Raynor. Her body had healed itself in the brief time she had been unconscious, and a few other things had also changed. Her Link to Nexus was back. She accessed as much data as she could to learn that the station was now falling through the upper atmosphere of Lunar. She tried to Link to Swift, but he didn't respond. Scanning the internal structure, she found Raynor and Jake in a power substation relatively close by. So, she figured they must have been working with Swift and Rob to fix something. Lisa leapt to her feet and sprinted to the substation. She wanted to try and help in any way she could. She felt like a fog had lifted from her mind and she wondered what had prevented her from being proactive about their predicament earlier.

Upon reaching her destination, Lisa quickly assessed the situation. Raynor was in direct contact with the power coupling. She could see the energy surging through his body. Jake was pounding at an interface and appeared to be trying desperately to shut it off, to no avail.

Lisa ran towards Raynor. If he were still alive, she could use her cybernetic enhancements to protect him by redirecting the power through herself. She knew there was a small chance it may burn her out also but didn't spare it a second thought. Instinct took over and she wrapped one arm around Raynor while placing her other hand on the coupling. It was like nothing else she had ever felt before. An immense energy flowed through them, the origin of which completely eluded her.

Appel pushed through the hordes of people that rushed frantically in all directions, searching for a ship to escape on. Everyone was pushing and shoving each other, trying to get ahead but no one was getting anywhere.

"Everyone back to the city. We need to get out of the docks," She yelled in vain. "No one is coming to save us!"

A man stopped her. He was huddled together with his family. "Are there really no more ships left? We're all done for?"

He just stood there waiting. She glanced down at his two young children who clutched frantically at their father's hands. They appeared tremendously scared.

"The station is about to crash into Lunar. We need to get back to the city. We will be safer there."

He looked at his family with uncertainty, picked his daughter up into his arms and pushed his way back towards the Transway, his partner and son following close behind. Appel could see the platform. People were piling off the carriages and spilling into the ship docks. All except for one. Her heart raced at the sight of Lazarus standing in the otherwise empty carriage.

"Lazarus!" she screamed at the top of her lungs. "Lazarus, wait!"

But there was no chance he could have heard her. She frantically pushed through the crowd, shoving at people who were getting in her path. The doors closed and the carriage surged into motion, carrying him away.

She looked back, relieved to see that a score of people had actually listened to her. Being the first one on, she instructed the carriage to take her to Aurora City. She had no idea which stop Lazarus would be going to. People crammed into the carriage after her. She wished they would hurry.

Within no time at all, the carriage was so packed that it groaned and rumbled as it lurched into motion. Appel wondered how the Transway would cope with so many people crammed into the relatively small space.

There was a chorus of electronic sounds as everyone's Link received an incoming communication. A woman's face was clearly visible on all the Links around her. Appel had never seen her before, but she appeared to be quite a young woman, with golden curls framing her immaculate face and intense blue eyes.

"People of Aurora. My name is Clarissa Dalton, daughter of Peacekeeper John Dalton. As you are aware, we are amid a crisis. The *M1 Orbital Space Station* is on a collision course towards Lunar. But please do not panic! We are working on a plan to land safely. This will not be an easy landing, but we have one of the Colonies top scientists working on it. If you are in the ship docks, please make your way back to the city. Moments before the impact we will divert all power to the artificial gravity matrix and the suspension field grid. You will feel a strong force holding you in place. Please do not resist it. This will dampen the impact. We can do this! We can survive!"

The carriage surged upward and gained speed as it shot vertically up the Transway path. Appel looked down on the thousands of people still in the ship docks as they erupted into motion. People tried to climb over each other in an attempt to get to safety. She wondered how many people would actually make it out and how many wouldn't.

Suddenly, the carriage jolted to a hard stop. The brakes screeched as they locked the carriage into place. People around her started to panic. Some of the lights flickered off leaving only the dull emergency lighting. She noticed almost straight away that it started to get harder to move, like the air was solidifying. She found herself gasping for air. She inhaled deeper and deeper, but she wasn't absorbing any oxygen in her lungs. There was a deep rumble that resonated through the walls. She squeezed her eyes shut, preparing for the worst. Then waited, and waited, but nothing happened. The rumbling got worse and the feeling of complete helplessness overwhelmed her.

She felt another force take hold of her. It was like a warm energy that ran through the entire station, and she felt connected with everyone in it. Like a warm hug from a protective parent, she could almost hear a voice repeating over and over that everything would be alright. But it was more of a feeling than a voice.

Then came the impact. Although she didn't move at all, the gravity felt like it had tripled, and she thought she would pass out from the inertia. The strain on her body was tremendous. The pressure kept building. She tried to scream but air wasn't moving through her lungs. Then, as quickly as it had begun, the weight was lifted and she could move once again. She fell straight to the floor, which left her looking down at the docks below. A quarter of it had caved in under the force of the impact and the entire structure was filling with water from the ocean outside. Thousands of people were now swimming for their lives or climbing onto anything that was still afloat, struggling to find a way to escape. She tried to get to her feet but the whole place was on a slant and she struggled to regain her balance.

She looked up when she heard a thump on the top of the carriage. A latch opened and her heart leapt when she saw Lazarus reaching down to her.

"Quickly, we need to get out of here," he said.

She wordlessly agreed by grabbing his hand, and he pulled her out of the carriage. He started to climb a service ladder to get back to the city.

"Wait, what about the rest of them?" She asked.

Lazarus looked at her for a moment and then let go of the rung he was holding onto.

"Alright, I can help them. But you start climbing. I'll see you at the top!"

He reached down and pulled out another passenger from inside the carriage. Appel started to climb up to the city surface. She was relieved to see it was only a few hundred metrons. Once she reached the top, she helped the others climbing behind her until finally she was reunited with Lazarus again. She was surprised when he embraced her in a hug, but she did not resist. Instead, she let the relief wash over her. "We need to keep moving," she said.

Lazarus grabbed her hand and led the way out of the building. Once out in the city, they were confronted by the utter destruction. The walls of the massive structure had disintegrated from the impact and the observation decks far above had collapsed into the city. She feared the worst for the rest of her crew but figured that they would have also been protected by the suspension field during the impact.

They spotted ships flying overhead and waved at them futilely. There were still so many people to rescue. The city surface began to flood with water as the station continued to sink.

"We need to get somewhere higher," Appel said, surveying the structures around them.

"How do you feel about heights?" Lazarus asked.

"Better than drowning."

"That building over there, with the webbed exostructure. That looks easy enough to climb. And tall enough that we'll be clearly visible."

Others had the same idea and were already scaling the side of the building. Appel led the way, placing one hand after another to keep a strong grip on the wall. She wanted to check that Lazarus was still right behind her, but she also didn't want to look down to see how far up they were. When they reached the top, she threw one leg over the ledge and pulled herself up to perch atop the structure. She looked out over the drowning city, the ocean breeze blew against her face and she took in a deep breath of salt air. Ships were dropping down to pick up groups of survivors.

Finally, it was their turn. The relief rushed through her as the opening of the shuttle lowered to the roof and a hand grasped at her outstretched fingers. It gripped hers firmly, pulling her up to safety. She shivered from the cold. Someone handed her a blanket, which Lazarus draped around her and cuddled up with her on the seat. She rested her head on his shoulder and closed her eyes.

Lisa and Raynor dropped to the floor as the gravity systems failed. They had been frozen in place by a suspension field and, for the entire span of the crash, could only stare silently into each other's eyes.

"Who *are* you?" Lisa asked groggily. "How were you able to survive all of that energy? Where did it even come from?"

"Are you delirious?" Raynor countered. "The energy came from *M1*. The power coupling was misaligned, so I had to correct it. If you hadn't come along when you did, I wouldn't have survived."

She knew the last part to be true, at least. Lisa was becoming accustomed to not getting a straight answer out of Raynor, but it still irritated her.

"You have it, don't you!" She insisted.

"Have what? Did that shock fry your circuits or something?"

Lisa jumped on top of Raynor and started frisking him in search of the item she suspected he was concealing.

"Get off me you crazy bitch!" Raynor shouted. He grabbed her wrists to stop her.

"You're trying to hide it! I know you are!"

Raynor let out a sigh and released her wrists reluctantly. "What is it exactly that you think I'm hiding?"

"The Artifact. You have it, don't you?" Lisa watched Raynor. She could feel his pulse, detect the smallest dilation in his iris'. She watched for any visual tell that would give away his secret.

"If you're quite finished feeling me up, I'd like to get out of here before this whole space station sinks into the ocean," Raynor suggested. Not a single shred of doubt in his voice.

Lisa had been defeated by Raynor once again. She dragged herself up to follow Raynor and Jake out of the sub-station.

Appel looked out over the wreckage and sheer destruction as they ascended. She realised the carnage didn't stop with *M1*; they were now high enough that she could see the nearby coastline flooded from the wave caused by the impact, and a line of destroyed skyscrapers that the space station had cut through on the way down.

Once the rescue ship landed on Lunar they were reunited with the rest of the crew. She looked around at her dishevelled crewmates. Rob, Raynor, Jake, even Lisa had made it off safely. They all looked a bit worse for wear, with cuts and scrapes all over them. Except for Lisa and Raynor who, despite their bloodied and battered clothing, appeared to be completely unharmed by the incident.

"Where are Persephone and Diputs?" Lazarus asked.

"Don't worry, they made it off before we entered the atmosphere," Rob assured him.

"What happens now?" Appel asked. "Did you find out how this all happened?"

"It would appear that it was an inside job," Rob responded. "If you ask me, Lunar looks pretty guilty. What with the Lunar Commander, June, having left the station right before. As soon as she found out it wouldn't burn up in the atmosphere, she was adamant to blow it up."

"I don't think it's that simple, Rob," Raynor said. "Something strange is going on here. Something just feels off about this whole thing."

"Well, that's for the Nexus to decide," Rob grumbled. "Not us. But I'm telling you, Lunar will get the blame. I, on the other hand, deserve to have something named after me."

Appel sat down next to Lazarus. Her hand found his and their fingers intertwined. It was finally all over.

DATAFILE

Encoded Message

Subject: Appointment of *M1* Orbital Space Station - Operational Team

As at C1098 S20 R24, Civic Armin has proven his value to the Colonies. Demonstrating that he has the skills and knowledge required to fill the role of a Station Operator and is hereby appointed to *M1* Orbital Space Station, effective immediately.

Signed,

Resden Koran

Foreseer of Lunar Colony Space-bound Operations

CHAPTER SIXTEEN

Aftermath

Swift relaxed into the large padded chair in his office. It was his favourite place to sit and think. He flicked through the reports on the interface in front of him, glad to see Lisa's name among the list of survivors, along with a great many others. His Link pulsed.

"Peacekeeper Dalton, so nice to see you alive and kicking."

"Yes, you too, Swift. I wanted to thank you for your efforts back there on *M1*. And for your continued assistance with the rescue and recovery of the survivors. Without your leadership and bravery none of us would have survived."

"Why, I was just doing my duty as Supreme Commander. Though I do hope in light of June Hellthorn's treachery there will be a serious inquiry regarding the conduct of the Lunar Colony and its representatives."

"June has been suspended pending a thorough investigation. You made the right call, Swift. I just want you to know, we will back you for it."

"That is comforting, thank you. Oh, and John, that deal your daughter made. You will honour it?"

Dalton paused. "We will. A deal is a deal."

With that final note, Dalton ended the Link. There was something still bothering Swift about the whole situation. He wanted to know how the outlaws could infiltrate the Colonies so easily. As if fate were answering his question, another message popped up on his interface.

SECURITY SYSTEM OVERRIDE: HOLDING BLOCK A

He flicked his interface across to the security visuals of the holding cells. The small containment quarters on Goliath housed twelve secure facilities. Diputs and Civic were the only people there. But the video link seemed a bit strange. He watched closely as the two men made the exact same movements every thirty seconds. Swift opened the live feed details and noticed that someone had hacked into it, causing it to playback false information.

"Come on now, that is the oldest trick around!" Swift murmured. He hacked back into the live feed. Instead of sending a security detail, he watched intently for what was about to unfold.

Diputs was resting his back against the padded bench. He just sat there, looking blankly into nothing. Swift watched him run his hand along the dark red projected wall and recoil from the electromagnetic forces of the suspension fields. The illumination of the cell walls flickered bleakly and then turned from red to aqua. Someone had unlocked them.

In the adjacent cell, the outlaw Civic was lying on the bench with his arm covering his eyes. He sat up and looked at Diputs. "This is it. We are finally going to meet our fate," he said, a desperate frantic tone in his voice.

"What are you going on about you fool?" Diputs demanded. "It's probably just mealtime. Or interrogation time. Either way, should be fun."

"You cared about Glitch? I mean Serena?" Civic asked.

"Yes, not that it is any of your business."

"Then I need you to do something for her. Recover her body and take it to her parents. You will find them on Pandora. As part of the Divine will, she must be laid to rest by her own kin."

Diputs hesitated briefly, fuming and muttering. Without any warning, he shouted. "You lied to Serena and tricked her into believing in your stupid Divine will. How dare you blatantly brainwash another individual like that, then ask me to respect your stupid customs? She is dead because of you!"

The cell doors flickered and then vanished. A formally dressed Lunar representative entered the containment area. Swift recognised the man as being Jackson Bainsby, the *M1* custodian.

"There. You're free to go," Bainsby said.

They each jumped up and headed for the door without question.

"Not you," Bainsby added. He grabbed Civic by the collar to stop him from going anywhere. "We need to have a little chat."

Diputs looked between the two of them and without further hesitation, took the opportunity that had been given him. Once Diputs had scurried out of the prison, Bainsby began his questioning. "What did you tell Swift about the mission?" He growled, then pushed Civic back down to the bench.

"Bainsby, my friend. Why would I tell him anything? We did exactly what you told us. Everything was going to plan and then, I don't know what went wrong."

"Nothing went wrong. You played your part well. It all went exactly to plan."

"You set us up for a suicide mission?"

"No, not a suicide mission. I mean if you had just stayed on board you probably would have been alright. Everything worked out in the end, didn't it? After all, I'm still here."

"Then why do all this?"

"You were part of a much larger plan, something bigger than you and I or your pitiful Divine god."

"What now then, you mad bastard? Are we going to destroy the Colonies? Because it sure as shit doesn't look like that's what you are doing."

"Have faith, my friend. I have faith in a higher power. Where is your faith?" Bainsby raised his blaster and pulled the trigger. A round of plasma energy burned a hole through Civic's head. The impact caused his innards to explode, splattering his brains around the prison. Some landed on Bainsby's face. He wiped it off with his sleeve and then left.

Swift sat forward in his chair, looking closer at the interface with a great deal of interest. His mind raced with what he had just witnessed. On the one hand, this cleared Diputs' name. On the other, Bainsby appeared to be not only connected with the outlaws but the mastermind behind this whole attack. He decided to watch the *M1* custodian for a little while, rather than turn him in right away. This plot sounded like it went a lot deeper than Bainsby, and Swift wanted to know just how deep.

BOOK THREE

Requiem

Reeling from the events on *M1* Space station, Diputs returns Serena's remains to her home on Enceladus (one of Saturn's moons). He confronts her grieving family and is then forced underground to 'help' them. Though his help is unwanted by some; discovering and embracing his true identity is the key to their survival. And while his crew work relentlessly to extract him from imminent danger, they too must reluctantly aid in his expedition in order to get back to *Galaxy* alive.

About The Author

Chris Masterton

 Chris is a space nerd, tech enthusiast, and sci-fi author. He enjoys exploring themes such as the future of humanity, artificial intelligence, and the impact technology has on society. Chris has a background in software and graphic design.

Connect with Chris:

- www.chrism.au

- goodreads.com/chrismasterton

About The Author

Steven Dutch

Steven Dutch was born in Auckland, New Zealand but grew up in Sydney, Australia. He would consider himself a foodie, and enjoys most cultures' foods. He works a day job as a Cyber Security Service Delivery Manager and enjoys everything scientific and technological, which bleeds over into his writing often. He has always been fascinated by science fiction and magic, thinking there is a fine line between the two and enjoys writing stories meshing and melding the two together. He has been writing for over 12 years and has completed several writing seminars and courses.

Connect with Steven:

- goodreads.com/stevendutch

History of Sol

History of Sol is an action/adventure sci-fi novella series set in the distant future.

Find out about the latest releases and where you can meet the authors using our social media links:

- historyofsol.com

- facebook.com/history.of.sol

- instagram.com/historyofsol

- twitter.com/historyofsol

Glossary

- **Enforcers:** Responsible for maintaining law and order

- **Foreseer:** Manages and assigns roles based on the needs of their Colony

- **Observer:** Spy/Intelligence gatherer

- **Peacekeeper:** The highest level of Nexus administration

- **Datafile:** An automated file system that gathers and sorts all information in the Nexus

- **Data Crystal:** A small quartz disk that serves as a mobile data storage device

- **Habitat:** A self-contained living area on smaller spacecraft

- **Interface:** Computer

- **Krontonium:** A rare element used to power the Star

- **Link:** Communication device / Mobile personal interface

- **Mitron:** Microscopic unit of measurement

- **Millitrons:** Tiny unit of measurement

- **Centron:** Small unit of measurement

- **Metron:** Medium unit of measurement

- **Kiltron:** Large unit of measurement

- **Nexus:**

- **a) name -** The governing body uniting all of the colonies under the 'Nexus Treaty'

- **b) technology -** A colony-wide shared communication and data system

- **Node:** A subsystem component of a Nexus or Datafile

- **Organix:** Liquid sustenance

- **Outlaw:** A general term used to denote people without Value

- **Robotoid:** A small self-mobilised robot

- **Rotation:** The time it takes for Mars to complete one rotation around its axis

- **Sub-Cycle:** 1/24th of a Cycle

- **Cycle:** The orbital period of Mars to pass once around Sol

- **Tectanium:** A super-strong metal derived from Titanium and enhanced with nano-tech

- **The Artifact:** A small shard of unknown material and origin

- **The Star:** A quantum state transference with a conduit of antimatter resonance (converts matter into light for brief periods of time)

- **The Terranean Expanse:** An asteroid belt between Lunar and Venus

- **Theridium Alpha:** A rare form of radioactive material found in the Kuiper belt

- **Unity:** A formal partnership between two or more people

- **Value:** Economic recognition based on contribution to a colony